THE GAME

Now, match w___
sulting detective___
completely succ___
be wise to keep in mind Holmes' advice to Watson
and all would-be detectives:

"It is an old maxim of mine," he said, "that when you have eliminated the impossible, whatever remains, however improbable, must be the truth."

Editorial Contributions: Kurt Fischer, Jessica Ney

Production: Terry K. Amthor, Richard H. Britton, Coleman Charlton, Kurt Fischer, Jessica Ney, John Ruemmler, Suzanne Young

Sherlock Holmes was created by the late Sir Arthur Conan Doyle and appears in novels and stories by him.

Grateful acknowledgment to Dame Jean Conan Doyle for permission to use the Sherlock Holmes characters created by Sir Arthur Conan Doyle.

PRINTED IN THE UNITED STATES OF AMERICA

Distributed by The Berkley Publishing Group, 200 Madison Avenue, New York, New York, 10016.

SHERLOCK HOLMES SOLO MYSTERIES™

MURDER
AT THE DIOGENES CLUB

by Gerald Lientz

Series Editor: John David Ruemmler
System Editor: S. Coleman Charlton
Cover Art &Illustrations by Daniel Horne

BERKLEY BOOKS, NEW YORK

CHARACTER RECORD

Name: JAMES G HURLEY

Skill	Bonus	Equipment:
Athletics	+1	1) notebook
Artifice	+1	2) pencil
Observation	+1	3) penknife
Intuition	+1	4)
Communication	+1	5)
Scholarship	+1	6)
		7)

Money: 10 pence · 8)
12 shillings · 9)
2 guineas · 10)
3 pounds · 11)

NOTES:

CHARACTER RECORD

Name:

Skill	Bonus	Equipment:
Athletics	_____	1)
Artifice	_____	2)
Observation	_____	3)
Intuition	_____	4)
Communication	_____	5)
Scholarship	_____	6)
		7)

Money:	_____pence	8)
	_____shillings	9)
	_____guineas	10)
	_____pounds	11)

NOTES:

CLUE SHEET

A _____

B _____

C _____

D _____

E _____

F _____

G _____

H _____

I _____

J _____

K _____

L _____

M _____

N _____

O _____

P _____

Q _____

R _____

S _____

T _____

U _____

V _____

W _____

X _____

Y _____

Z _____

Deductions & Decisions Sheet

1 _____
2 _____
3 _____
4 _____
5 _____
6 _____
7 _____
8 _____
9 _____
10 _____
11 _____
12 _____
13 _____
14 _____
15 _____
16 _____
17 _____
18 _____
19 _____
20 _____
21 _____
22 _____
23 _____
24 _____
25 _____

AN INTRODUCTION TO THE WORLD OF SHERLOCK HOLMES

HOLMES AND WATSON

First appearing in "A Study in Scarlet" in Beeton's Christmas Annual of 1887, Sherlock Holmes remains a remarkably vigorous and fascinating figure for a man of such advanced years. The detective's home and office at 221B Baker Street are shrines now, not simply rooms in which Holmes slept and deduced and fiddled with the violin when he could not quite discern the significance of a clue or put his finger on a criminal's twisted motive.

We know both a great deal and very little about Sherlock Holmes as a person. The son of a country squire (and grandson of the French artist Vernet's sister), Holmes seems to have drawn little attention to himself until his University days, where his extraordinary talents for applying logic, observation and deduction to solving petty mysteries earned him a reputation as something of a genius. Taking the next logical step, Holmes set up a private consulting detective service, probably in 1878. Four years later, he met and formed a partnership with a former military surgeon, Dr. John Watson. Four novels and fifty-six short stories tell us everything we know of the odd pair and their extraordinary adventures.

Less a well-rounded individual than a collection of contradictory and unusual traits, Holmes seldom exercised yet was a powerful man of exceptional speed of foot. He would eagerly work for days on a case with no rest and little food, yet in periods of idleness would refuse to get out of bed for days. Perhaps his most telling comment appears in "The Adventure of the Mazarin Stone:"

I am a brain, Watson. The rest of me is a mere appendix.

Holmes cared little for abstract knowledge, once noting that it mattered not to him if the earth circled the sun or vice versa. Yet he could identify scores of types of tobacco ash or perfume by sight and odor, respectively. Criminals and their modus operandi obsessed him; he pored over London's sensational newspapers religiously.

A master of disguise, the detective successfully presented himself as an aged Italian priest, a drunken groom, and even an old woman! A flabbergasted Watson is the perfect foil to Holmes, who seems to take special delight in astonishing his stuffy if kind cohort.

In "The Sign of Four," Holmes briefly noted the qualities any good detective should possess in abundance (if possible, intuitively): heightened powers of observation and deduction, and a broad range of precise (and often unusual) knowledge. In this ***Sherlock Holmes Solo Mysteries***™ adventure, you will have ample opportunity to test yourself in these areas, and through replaying the adventure, to improve your detective skills.

Although impressive in talent and dedication to his profession, Sherlock Holmes was by no means perfect. Outfoxed by Irene Adler, Holmes readily acknowledged defeat by "the woman" in "A Scandal in Bohemia." In 1887, he admitted to Watson that three men had outwitted him (and Scotland Yard). The lesson Holmes himself drew from these failures was illuminating:

> *Perhaps when a man has special knowledge and special powers like my own, it rather encourages him to seek a complex explanation when a simpler one is at hand.*

So learn to trust your own observations and deductions — when they make sense and match the physical evidence and the testimony of trusted individuals — don't rush to judgment, and if you like and the adventure allows, consult Holmes or Watson for advice and assistance.

VICTORIAN LONDON

When Holmes lived and worked in London, from the early 1880's until 1903, the Victorian Age was much more than a subject of study and amusement. Queen Victoria reigned over England for more than 60 years, an unheard of term of rule; her tastes and inhibitions mirrored and formed those of English society. Following the Industrial Revolution of roughly 1750-1850, England leaped and stumbled her way from a largely pastoral state into a powerful, flawed factory of a nation. (The novels of Charles Dickens dramatically depict this cruel, exhilarating period of sudden social change.) Abroad, imperialism planted the Union Jack (and implanted English mores) in Africa, India, and the Far East, including Afghanistan, where Dr. Watson served and was wounded.

Cosmopolitan and yet reserved, London in the late Nineteenth Century sported over six million inhabitants, many from all over the world; it boasted the high society of Park Lane yet harbored a seedy Chinatown where opium could be purchased and consumed like tea. To orient yourself, you should note that Baker Street is located just south of Regent's Park, near the Zoological Gardens, in the heart of the stylish West End of the city. Railway and horse-drawn carriages were the preferred means of transport; people often walked, and thieves frequently ran to get from one place to another.

THE GAME'S AFOOT!

Now, match wits with the world's greatest consulting detective. And have no fear — if you don't completely succeed at first, just play again! It might be wise to keep in mind Holmes' advice to Watson and all would-be detectives:

> *"It is an old maxim of mine," he said, "that when you have eliminated the impossible, whatever remains, however improbable, must be the truth."*

Good luck and good hunting!

THE *SHERLOCK HOLMES SOLO MYSTERIES*™ GAME SYSTEM

THE GAMEBOOK

This gamebook describes hazards, situations, and locations that may be encountered during your adventures. As you read the text sections, you will be given choices as to what actions you may take. What text section you read will depend on the directions in the text and whether the actions you attempt succeed or fail.

Text sections are labeled with three-digit numbers (e.g.,"365"). Read each text section only when told to do so by the text.

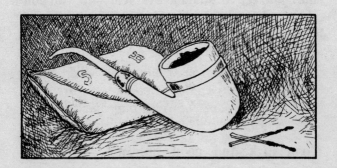

PICKING A NUMBER

Many times during your adventures in this game-book you will need to pick a number (between 2 and 12). There are several ways to do this:

1) Turn to the Random Number Table at the end of this book, use a pencil (or pen or similar object), close your eyes, and touch the Random Number Table with the pencil. The number touched is the number which you have picked. If your pencil falls on a line, just repeat the process. **or**

2) Flip to a random page in the book and look at the small boxed number in the inside, bottom corner of the page. This number is the number which you have picked. **or**

3) If you have two six-sided dice, roll them. The result is the number which you have picked. (You can also roll one six-sided die twice and add the results.)

Often you will be instructed to pick a number and add a "bonus". When this happens, treat results of more than 12 as "12" and treat results of less than 2 as "2".

INFORMATION, CLUES, AND SOLVING THE MYSTERY

During play you will discover certain clues (e.g., a footprint, murder weapon, a newspaper article) and make certain decisions and deductions (e.g., you decide to follow someone, you deduce that the butler did it). Often the text will instruct you to do one of the following:

Check Clue xx or *Check Decision xx* or *Check Deduction xx.*

"xx" is a letter for Clues and a number for Decisions and Deductions. When this occurs, check the appropriate box on the "Clue Record Sheets" found at the beginning of the book. You should also record the information gained and note the text section number on the line next to the box. You may copy or photocopy these sheets for your own use.

Other useful information not requiring a "check" will also be included in the text. You may want to take other notes, so a "NOTES" space is provided at the bottom of your "Character Record". Remember that some of the clues and information given may be meaningless or unimportant (i.e., red herrings).

EQUIPMENT AND MONEY

Whenever you acquire money and equipment, record them on your Character Record in the spaces provided. Pennies (1 Pence), shillings (12 pence), guineas (21 shillings), and pounds (20 shillings) are "money" and may be used during your adventures to pay for food, lodging, transport, bribes, etc. Certain equipment may affect your abilities as indicated by the text.

You begin the adventure with the money noted on the completed Character Record sheet near the front of the book.

CHOOSING A CHARACTER

There are two ways to choose a character:

1) You can use the completely created character provided at the beginning of the book. **or**
2) You can create your own character using the simple character development system included in the next section of this book.

STARTING TO PLAY

After reading the rules above and choosing a character to play, start your adventures by reading the Prologue found after the rules section. From this point on, read the passages as indicated by the text.

CREATING YOUR OWN CHARACTER

If you do not want to create your own character, use the pre-created character found in the front of this book. If you decide to create your own character, follow the directions given in this section. Keep track of your character on the blank Character Record found in the front of this book. It is advisable to enter information in pencil so that it can be erased and updated. If necessary, you may copy or photocopy this Character Record for your own use.

As you go through this character creation process, refer to the pre-created character in the front of the book as an example.

SKILLS

The following 6 "Skill Areas" affect your chances of accomplishing certain actions during your adventures.

1) **Athletics** (includes fitness, adroitness, fortitude, pugnacity, fisticuffs): This skill reflects your ability to perform actions and maneuvers requiring balance, coordination, speed, agility, and quickness. Such actions can include fighting, avoiding attacks, running, climbing, riding, swimming, etc.

2) **Artifice** (includes trickery, disguise, stealth, eavesdropping): Use this skill when trying to move without being seen or heard (i.e., sneaking), trying to steal something, picking a lock, escaping from bonds, disguising yourself, and many other similar activities.

3) **Intuition** (includes sensibility, insight, reasoning, deduction, luck): This skill reflects your ability to understand and correlate information, clues, etc. It also reflects your ability to make guesses and to have hunches.

4) **Communication** (includes interviewing, acting, mingling, negotiating, diplomacy): This skill reflects your ability to talk with, negotiate with, and gain information from people. It also reflects your "social graces" and social adaptivity, as well as your ability to act and to hide your own thoughts and feelings.

5) Observation (includes perception, alertness, empathy): This skill reflects how much information you gather through visual perception.

6) Scholarship (includes education, science, current events, languages): This skill reflects your training and aptitude with various studies and sciences: foreign languages, art, history, current events, chemistry, tobaccory, biology, etc.

SKILL BONUSES

For each of these skills, you will have a Skill Bonus that is used when you attempt certain actions. When the text instructs you to "add your bonus," it is referring to these Skill Bonuses. Keep in mind that these "bonuses" can be negative as well as positive.

When you start your character, you have six "+1 bonuses" to assign to your skills.

You may assign more than one "+1 bonuses" to a given skill, but no more than three to any one skill. Thus, two "+1 bonuses" assigned to a skill will be a "+2 bonus", and three "+1 bonuses" will be a "+3 bonus". Each of these bonuses should be recorded in the space next to the appropriate skill on your Character Record.

If you do not assign any "+1 bonuses" to a skill, you must record a "-2 bonus" in that space.

During play you may acquire equipment or injuries that may affect your bonuses. Record these modifications in the "Bonus" spaces.

Cast of Characters

Pierre Armand: French wine and spirits dealer.

Sir Alexander Bassett-Hynde: Historian and member of the Diogenes Club.

Bowser and Fitzhugh: Gamblers.

Henry Hamilton: Solicitor who handed Colonel Sylvester a letter before his death.

Lord Hampton: Wealthy owner of racehorses.

Mycroft Holmes: Member of the Diogenes Club, brother to Sherlock.

Irish Star: Well thought-of racehorse.

The Honorable Charles Martin: Member of Parliament and of the Diogenes Club.

Admiral William Nelson: Member of the Diogenes Club.

John Oliver: Irish Star's groom.

Henry Raines: Irish Star's trainer.

Roscoe: Proprietor of gambling operation.

Sir Andrew St. James: Chairman of the Diogenes Club.

Tom Smithson: Waiter at the Diogenes Club.

Stanly: A Baker Street irregular.

Colonel Ian Stuart: Owner of Irish Star.

Colonel Philip Sylvester: Recently-deceased member of the Diogenes Club.

Lord Trent: Merchant and member of the Diogenes Club.

PROLOGUE

On a pleasant summer day in London, you decide to visit your mentor, Sherlock Holmes, and your cousin, Dr. John Watson. Perhaps today Mr. Holmes will hand you a case to solve yourself.

Upon reaching 221B Baker Street, Mrs. Hudson admits you with a smile, although obviously in the midst of a busy cleaning session. "How nice to see you again," says Holmes' landlady. "Mr. Holmes and Doctor Watson are in their rooms. You know the way."

"Yes ma'am," you reply, turning toward the stair.

"You might do me a favor," she continues. You pause at the words. "Dr. Watson's newspaper just came; it would save a trip if you'd take it with you. I just came down from carrying the doctor a telegram, and I've a thousand things to do today."

Naturally, you agree. At your knock, Mr. Holmes invites you in, and both men greet you brusquely. Doctor Watson sits at his desk, writing, a telegram sticking out of his vest pocket. His pipe drawing well, Holmes relaxes near the window. After returning their greetings, you hand your cousin his newspaper and sit to talk with Holmes. Although rarely given easily, the detective's thoughts are always worth hearing. As you talk, you notice Watson turn to the back page of his paper, look at it intently for a moment, and then toss it aside with a grunt of disgust.

Holmes chuckles. "You're quite right, Watson. You will make more money telling the story of Silver Blaze than betting any of tomorrow's races."

"That's what I decided, Holmes," Watson replies. "Those horses would have trouble — how did you know what I was thinking?"

"I knew the same way I always know," Holmes replies. "By observation and reasoning. Besides, Watson, you make so much from my analysis of the trivial that you hardly have the right to complain."

"All right, Holmes, the point is well taken," Watson agrees, blushing as he smiles. "But for the life of me, I don't see how you did it this time. I hadn't even told you that I was writing one of your adventures, much less which case."

"Very well, Watson, I shall explain." Holmes pauses. "No, I have a better idea. Our young friend here will retrace my steps and show us how well he has studied my techniques. Come now, see what you can do. I shall provide a little guidance."

Suddenly nervous, you marshal your thoughts, trying to remember every significant detail of the morning.

"Where shall I start?" you ask, stalling for time.

"Why don't you try the telegram first?" Holmes suggests. "Just before you arrived, Watson received a telegram which he stuck in his pocket without reading. What does that suggest to you?"

"That he was in a hurry," you reply, covering your mouth in dismay at speaking without thinking. "No, how could he be in a hurry when he's sitting at his desk? It must be something else." *Pick a number and add your Intuition bonus:*

- *If 2-6, turn to 323.*
- *If 7-12, turn to 638.*

101

"Exactly what are the rules of the Club regarding behaviour and application for membership?" you ask.

Sir Andrew relaxes; he is on firmer ground here. "No talking is permitted anywhere in the members' area of the club, except for the area we call the outsiders' room. Naturally, I occasionally give orders to the staff, and they are permitted to talk — strictly in the line of duty, in their work areas. We pay them well to see that they obey.

"As for membership rules," Sir Andrew continues, "we are perhaps more liberal than some clubs. This is an expensive establishment, and it is not to every man's taste. On the other hand, as members need not associate with each other, we are tolerant of each other. Provided a man does nothing to disturb the club itself, our members accept him. Indeed, Mr. Sherlock Holmes was one of the more hotly disputed members permitted to join, because of his public position and the sometimes resultant noise. It was only his longtime good behaviour as a guest, and our great respect for his brother Mycroft that resulted in his election." *Turn to 379.*

102

"I am curious," you begin, "how you came to hand a note to the Colonel. It hardly seems the duty of a solicitor."

"On the contrary," he laughs, "it is a most natural task if the writer desires the delivery to be most discreet. I recently returned from abroad, and I am trying to build a practice, so the fee for such a commission is very useful. A man I did not know came to my office, explained that he had some very important information for the Colonel, but that he would prefer I deliver the warning."

"Warning?" you ask eagerly.

"'Warning' is what he called it," Hamilton replies. "It was a sealed envelope, but with Colonel Sylvester's reputation, it seemed hardly unusual for him to be receiving some kind of warning." *Check Clue Y.*

- *If you ask about the note, turn to 215.*
- *Otherwise, turn to 420.*

103

"I know," you begin, "that no horseman likes to lose a race at any time, especially under suspicious circumstances."

Colonel Stuart nods.

"However, sir," you continue, "I wonder whether so prosaic a matter as losing the purse money from the race might have a damaging effect upon your stable."

Stuart bristles for a moment, then nods. "Fair enough. I suppose you need to know, although it's humiliating to a man of my rank to discuss such things."

"Yes, I do," you say encouragingly.

"Then, in simple language," Colonel Stuart admits, "losing that purse today may ruin me. The only reason that I entered Irish Star against such weak competition was to win the purse and to pay my bills. Now, I shall have to sell Irish Star, and perhaps my stable as well." The Colonel's square shoulders slump as he contemplates the disaster. **Check Clue B. Pick a number** and add your Intuition bonus:

• If 2-5, **turn to 376.**
• If 6-12, **turn to 487.**

104

"Did you obtain a sample from Colonel Sylvester's bottle at the Club Bar?" Holmes asks.

• If you have checked Clue N, **turn to 375.**
• Otherwise, **turn to 143.**

105

You stand poised to search Colonel Stuart's stables.

• If you search the groom's room, **turn to 197.**
• if you search Irish Star's stall, **turn to 455.**
• If you search the tackroom, **turn to 404.**

106

"There's someone in there, Watson," you whisper. "We must do something! Help me force the door."

Watson looks at the door and shakes his head. "We would need an ax to break that door in," he whispers. "Can't you work the lock? Besides, the porter would summon the police if we broke in the door, and we would be hard put to justify our action."

"I don't know if I can pick the lock," you say, "but I shall try!" **Pick a number** and add your Artifice bonus:

• If 2-7, **turn to 464.**
• if 8-12, **turn to 473.**

107

"Do you have a list of those who bought that brandy?" you ask the man. **Pick a number** and add your Communication bonus:

• If 2-6, **turn to 498.**
• If 7-12, **turn to 535.**

108

Rather than searching the buildings along the alley, you hide in a doorway where you can watch from the front. You remain so for a long time, and Watson grows impatient beside you. Half an hour passes without a sign of Hamilton. Perhaps you should have searched the buildings after all.

●*If you search the first building, a grocer's storeroom,* **turn to 558.**
●*If you search the second, a cellar,* **turn to 561.**
●*If you search the third, a vacant tavern,* **turn to 194.**
●*If you continue to wait,* **turn to 271.**

109

You carefully review the evidence to Holmes, hoping that the detective will agree that you have proved Hamilton's guilt.

●*If you checked Clue Q,* **turn to 525.**
●*Otherwise,* **turn to 531.**

110

You survey Watson's desk point-by-point. Envelopes, stamps and other supplies fill the slots along the raised back. A pile of hand-written sheets lies at the left side, while blank paper is handy on the right. Watson pretends to write on a sheet, perhaps to recreate the scene. Three crumpled balls of paper are scattered around his feet. *Turn to 435.*

111

You consider the report that Lord Hampton tried to buy Irish Star for a small price.

●*If you ask him about it,* **turn to 493.**
●*If not,* **turn to 317.**

112

"I think Colonel Sylvester's valet killed him," you hesitantly assert. "He intensely despised Sylvester." You describe the man's behaviour at Sylvester's flat.

"The valet could hardly have done it," Holmes answers. "It is unlikely that a man of his position would learn of the drug, and there simply is no evidence suggesting that he carried out the crime." *Turn to 296.*

113

You find that Hamilton is too strong for you and cannot even yell for help as his last blow knocks you out.

Slowly you awake, feeling someone wiping your face and neck with cold water. When you pry your eyes open you see Watson's anxious face bent over you, as he tends your bruises.

"How long was I out?" you ask.

"Half an hour or more," he replies. "I decided I'd waited long enough and found you lying here. Hamilton is long gone, I'm afraid." *Turn to 409.*

114

Colonel Stuart looks at you with pronounced distaste. "Are they letting you blunder your way through another case, after the hash you made when my horse was drugged?" You can think of no reply as he continues. "It is fortunate that no real crime took place here, for the sake of justice."

•*If you checked Deduction 12, turn to 175.*
•*Otherwise, turn to 350.*

115

Holmes listens intently to your explanation and gives the briefest of approving nods. "Given Hamilton's presence when Sylvester died, the note by itself is probably evidence enough," he admits, "but it would be far more profitable to provide evidence establishing his motives for the crime, as well as some West Indian background linking Hamilton, however circumstantially, to the drug. But you have solved the case." *Turn to 539.*

116

"Now may I read the list of bets?" you demand of Roscoe's clerk.

"C-C-Certainly, sir," the man stutters, cringing. You look over the book and are surprised to find that no one bet heavily on Maiwand or any of Irish Star's competitors. As you think about this, Watson urges you to leave the area.

"Come," he mutters, "I must catch a train. Colonel Stuart is waiting for you now." When you agree, your cousin hurries off. *Turn to 228.*

117

You search your memory, then remember hearing of the brandy before. Only one dealer in London, Amber's, imports that brand. *Check Clue M. Turn to 609.*

118

"I believe that Sylvester's French rival, Pierre Armand, committed the murder," you say. "It is too remarkable a coincidence to find a man ruined by Sylvester, with the West Indian background (and thus access to the fatal drug) who is also the man responsible for the importation of Sylvester's brandy."

"No, no," Holmes chides."How could he have gotten the drug into the brandy? Think. He would not dare drug every bottle, just because Colonel Sylvester drinks it. Armand's motive is quite weak, I should say, and the method you suggest — impossible!" *Turn to 296.*

119

You wonder if any problems arise in the club from personal enmity among the members. With no chance to vent disagreements through an occasional argument, hostility could rise to the point where it might lead to almost any result. Could any of the members in the lounge with Colonel Sylvester have had a particular reason to dislike him?

•*If you ask about other members in the lounge with Colonel Sylvester,* **turn to 366.**

•*Otherwise,* **turn to 499.**

120

"I think the waiter, Tom Smithson, murdered the Colonel," you tell Holmes. "To revenge his brother's death."

Holmes shakes his head, looking askance at you much as he looks at Watson on occasion. "There simply is no evidence to support that conclusion," he says, "no evidence at all. If a man of Smithson's class were going to commit a murder, he would do it with a club or knife, not with an odd drug that kills indirectly, no?" ***Turn to 296.***

121

You decide to stick to your original plan and ride the Express to Bristol. There you get a couple of local police to help, but when the local train arrives, Hamilton does not exit it. A thorough search proves he is hiding nowhere on the train. *Turn to 409.*

122

You thank the bartender for his help and leave the bar.

As you turn into the hall, Watson asks, "Well, are you going to read that note or aren't you?"

You realize that you still have the envelope in your hand. *Turn to 587.*

123

"I was all ready to follow that bloke Oliver you set me on," Stanly says breathlessly, "but then I seen him carried off by the coppers. It didn't seem much use followin' then, so I come away." You give him a coin and thank him. *Turn to 129.*

124

"I saw that man slip out of the stables with some water pails," Stanly goes on, "but he dropped them and doubled back behind the stable. Then he felt 'round back of one of the window shutters and took somethin' out. It was too small for me to see what he 'ad, so I just kept followin' him. Finally, acting real sneaky, he went way around behind the refreshment stand, and then I see him toss this little bottle into the trash heap back of the stand." He hands you a small medicine bottle labeled: "HASTINGS DISTILLATE OF OPIUM." *Check Clue H. Pick a number and add your Scholarship bonus:*

●*If 2-5, turn to 398.*
●*If 6-9, turn to 200.*
●*If 10-12, turn to 255.*

125

Holmes looks stunned. "Are you serious?" he asks. *Turn to 999.*

126

"After you found the medicine bottle, did you see Oliver do anything else?" you ask Stanly. *Pick a number.*

●*If 2-7, turn to 418.*
●*If 8-12, turn to 340.*

127

You don't make a sound as you search the celler of the abandoned pub. Suddenly, you hear a low coughing in a corner, and remember Hamilton's health problem. You edge towards the sound and find

Hamilton, who is crouched between two barrels. You jump him before he knows you are there. *Turn to 612.*

128

"You think that I wrote this?" he demands.

When you nod, he snorts loudly, muttering: "And I thought you had some brains. Bloody idiot. My name is Ian Stuart, not Henry. Well, do you have any other nonsense to waste my time with?" *Turn to 350.*

129

Slowly you finish your dinner, contemplating what you have learned.

•*If you checked Clue H, turn to 551.*
•*Otherwise, turn to 480.*

130

You smile at Mycroft, trying to think of the best way to ask your questions.

•*If you ask what he thought of Sylvester, turn to 136.*
•*Otherwise, turn to 658.*

131

Holmes smiles vaguely as you finish your explanation of the crime. "There is hope for your cousin, Watson. He certainly has the potential to make a good detective; although he failed to uncover every relevant clue, he put together a solid case."

•*If you want Holmes' help, turn to 546.*
•*If you want to try again to solve the mystery on your own, turn to 237.*

132

As you bend over the list, Roscoe grabs your shoulder and yells: "Just what do you think you're doing, mate? Now get away from this or I'll teach you what snoops get!" He shakes his big fist in your face.

•*If you leave, turn to 228.*
•*If you fight Roscoe, turn to 618.*

133

"I must go, now that you're finished with me," Holmes says, consulting his watch. "Take proper care tonight; perhaps good fortune will result. One never knows. Come to Baker Street tomorrow morning and tell me what you have found." As you nod, the detective hurries away.

Sir Andrew St. James takes you in his charge. "We will give you every assistance we can," he begins. "I hope you can bring this dreadful matter to a swift and quiet conclusion. If you want to see the actual body, you had better do so now. There are men waiting to take it away already. Otherwise, I shall bring in those who might know something useful."

"Who are the witnesses?" you ask.

"There are ten," he answers. "I regret keeping so many waiting, but the Colonel's death was so sudden that it seems very odd. I realize that due to my position, you may wish to ask me a few questions. In addition to me, there were six members of the club in the lounge where the Colonel died. You have talked with Mr. Sherlock Holmes already, but his brother Mycroft was present also; Sir Alexander Bassett-Hynde, the noted historian; the Honourable Charles Martin, M.P.; Lord Trent, the merchant and industrialist; and Admiral William Nelson were also in the room. A solicitor, Mr. Henry Hamilton, delivered a note to Colonel Sylvester this afternoon, while Colonel Ian Stuart, Colonel Sylvester's cousin and heir, came to see him. I understand that Colonel Sylvester refused to talk with his cousin. In addition, I have asked Tom Smithson, who was serving the members in the small lounge, remain in case you want to ask him anything."

•*If you see the body, turn to 253.*
•*If you begin interviewing witnesses now, turn to 181.*

134

The final item of interest is an envelope sitting on the table beside Colonel Sylvester's chair.

"That was delivered to the Colonel just before he died," Sir Andrew says. "He did not look at it."

Watson picks up the note. "It would be just as well to look at it," he says. "Holmes always says you should never ignore any piece of evidence, however ordinary. That's odd," he adds, glancing at it as he passes it on to you.

You read the address before responding. There is a 13 in the lefthand corner of the envelope. The address reads:

Colonel A. J. Sylvester
At the Diogenes
Fleet Street, London

"What's odd, Doctor?" you ask, weighing the note in your hand.

"Why, the address," Watson replies. "We are on Pall Mall, not Fleet Street."

"The address can hardly matter as the note was delivered by hand," Sir Andrew suggests. "Now, would you like to talk to the bartender who worked this afternoon? If not, I have something for him to do."

•*If you see the bartender, turn to 465.*
•*Otherwise, turn to 587.*

You tell Holmes how Oliver was paid off by Roscoe, apparently without placing a wager, and Holmes gives a curt nod. "That's likely enough evidence to indict the rogue," he says. "Oliver, at the very least, must have told Roscoe that the horse would run badly. It would have been preferable to show that Oliver had possession of the drug. But I am certain that your solution is the correct one."

•*If you want to try to solve the mystery again without being given the solution,* **turn to the Prologue** *and begin anew.*

•*Otherwise,* **turn to 460.**

"What did you think of Colonel Sylvester?" you ask. "What sort of man was he?"

Mycroft stares at you for a moment before replying, perhaps wondering if you will ever ask anything of import. "I cannot say that I liked the man, but I cannot say I hated him. He was terribly ordinary — he customarily sought the easy way to do things — not a great man, but adequate if not pressed hard."

You sigh, wondering if anyone will give you a straight answer. *Turn to 658.*

"Excuse me, Doctor," you begin, "but a friend gave me a vial of horse medicine, and I thought I'd get some expert opinion before I use it." You hand him the bottle and wait as he stares owlishly at it. Finally, he begins to say something.

"I didn't know there was any of this left in the country," he mutters, "seeing as there never was much of it. Dr. Hastings was a good horse doctor who liked to experiment. He mixed this up as something to calm wild horses but died before he could decide how well it worked. Only a few friends of his ever used it, and no one ever found the formula. I'm very surprised to see it at a track, I can tell you. It's something you'd use back home at the farm." *Pick a number and add your Intuition bonus:*

•*If 2-8,* **turn to 480.**
•*If 9-12,* **turn to 306.**

"Aye, I guess it might look a little odd to you," the jockey says, "but it's a habit of mine. I ride many and many a different horse each day, you see. Some of them are a little unfriendly, and a morsel makes them more willing to have me aboard. Sometimes, with a horse like Irish Star was today, I think a bite wakes them up a bit. The horse was dead on his hooves when I warmed him up. Didn't do no good though, as you saw." He turns away and waves for the bartended to serve more drinks, ignoring you. *Turn to 439.*

The idea that Hamilton used a boat to double back down the Thames appeals to you, and you send a telegraph to the authorities in Greenwich to watch for him. By the time you have confirmation that they will do this, the Bristol Express has come and gone.

You and Watson hurry to his club to await the results and are having tea when the telegraph arrives. No man similar to Hamilton was seen on the boat at Greenwich. *Turn to 409.*

140

"Colonel Stuart's groom, John Oliver, drugged Irish Star," you say with confidence, a feeling that increases when you see Holmes nod in agreement.

Then Holmes says, "What evidence do you have?" You must explain your findings. The relevant proof includes Clues F, H, and I and Deduction 10.

•*If you have checked Clue F only,* **turn to 332**
•*If you have checked Deduction 10, but not Clues H or I, turn to 470.*

•*If you have checked Clue H but not I, turn to 571.*
•*If you have checked Clue I but not H, turn to 135.*
•*If you have checked Clues H and I, turn to 500.*

141

With a thrill of delight, you feel your arms wrap around the murderer's legs and trip him up. He turns to punch you, but stops immediately. Watson is there, his service revolver commanding Hamilton's obedience. *Turn to 613.*

142

"The men I saw are gamblers," Holmes explains. "They've been implicated in one or two races that had odd results, though no charges could be proven in court. I wasn't asked to look into the cases, as it happens. But even if it were impossible for the Jockey Club to warn them off the turf entirely, I'm surprised anyone would allow them near the horses. The gentlemanly one is named Fitzhugh, while his partner is called Bowser."

Watson leads the way to one of the low hills between stables and track and shakes out a blanket for the three of you to sit on. "I always sit here," Watson explains.

"A lucky seat?" Holmes asks sardonically, as he sits down.

Watson tries to wither Holmes with a look. "Luck has nothing to do with it, Holmes. This gives us a good view as the horses warm up and is convenient to the wagering tables."

The truth of this observation is proven during the early races. Watson takes full advantage of the convenient location, with a success that has him crowing with delight. *Pick a number and add your Intuition bonus:*

- *If 2-5, turn to 363.*
- *If 6-12, turn to 384.*

143

You shake your head, embarrassed at neglecting this step.

"The bottle, Holmes?" Watson asks. "What possible good would the bottle do? The Colonel was drinking from the glass."

Holmes withers him with a stare. "If the drug were already in the bottle, Watson, it would mean that a larger, and perhaps different, group of men had the chance to poison Colonel Sylvester."

- *If you checked Clue R, turn to 169.*
- *Otherwise, turn to 157.*

144

"Lord Hampton was responsible for the drugging," you state firmly. "His connection with the drug marks him — none of the other suspects had easy access to it."

"Well-reasoned," Holmes admits. "It would have been wiser to find a motive as well, but the evidence you present is sound. Now, we must decide how to deal with his Lordship, who will arrive within a few minutes."

- *If you want to try to solve the mystery again without being given the solution, turn to the Prologue and begin anew.*
- *Otherwise, turn to 185.*

145

Holmes looks at you in astonishment and disgust as you name the party whom you believe drugged the horse. "No, no," he sighs. "I am grossly disappointed in you."

- *If you want to try again, turn to the Prologue and begin anew.*
- *Otherwise, turn to 148.*

146

"What happened to your brother, may I ask?" you inquire encouragingly.

"Aye, sir, my brother John. He were killed in India, in the Colonel's command, oh, ten or more years back."
Check Clue P.

- *If you ask more about the Colonel, turn to 386.*
- *Otherwise, turn to 269.*

147

You wonder whether it is coincidence that Sylvester's old enemy, Pierre Armand, happened to be in London on the day of the murder.

●*If you visit Pierre Armand at his hotel,* **turn to 556.**
●*Otherwsie,* **turn to 349.**

148

"If you had really thought through the evidence," Holmes says, lighting his pipe, "I think it obvious that the groom, John Oliver, gave the drug to the horse." **Turn to 621.**

149

Holmes shakes his head, obviously disappointed, as you answer the question. "No, no," he says, "how can you fail to point the finger where it belongs?"

●*If you want to try again,* **turn to the Prologue***and begin anew.*
●*Otherwise,* **turn to 156.**

150

"I think Lord Hampton is guilty," you say. "Irish Star's impressive workout made his Lordship jealous."

Holmes' faint smile fades into a frown. "That is more a guess than a matter of physical evidence," the detective says. "You need proof! Lord Hampton is coming here soon, and we must agree upon a course of action that guarantees Colonel Stuart justice."

●*If you want to try to solve the mystery again without being given the solution,* **turn to the Prologue***and begin anew.*

●*Otherwise,* **turn to 185.**

151

"Why did you come to see Colonel Sylvester?" you ask. **Pick a number** *and add your Communication bonus:*

●*If 2-8,* **turn to 280.**
●*If 9-12,* **turn to 530.**

152

"Whatever the poison, it killed him quick enough," you mutter.

"Yes, yes indeed," Watson answers, still a little shaken. "I am certain that Holmes has a tome describing the poisons which yield such an effect." **Turn to 445.**

153

You feel Hamilton's bullet jerk at your coattail, but you dive into the brush and wrestle him to the ground. His gun is knocked away. Before he can fight back, Watson appears, his gun very visible. Quickly you tie Hamilton's hands. **Turn to 613.**

You walk to a pub near the track, where Holmes instructed the irregular to meet you. While you wait, you order supper. As you eat, you see Irish Star's jockey enter boisterously and order a round of drinks for a group of men who entered with him.

•*If you talk to the jockey,* **turn to 437.**
•*Otherwise,* **turn to 439.**

155

Holmes shakes his head, obviously disappointed, as you answer the question. "No, no," he says, "how can you fail to point the finger where it belongs?"

•*If you want to try again,* **turn to the Prologue** *and begin anew.*
•*Otherwise,* **turn to 156.**

156

"I should have thought that the guilt of Lord Hampton was obvious to all," Holmes sums up, blowing blue smoke toward the lights.

"Oh, be patient, Holmes," Watson laughs. "He shall learn. Even you were misled once or twice, when you were younger."

The detective looks sharply at his friend, then chuckles. "I shall have to watch you, Watson. You age well, like fine wine." With a few more courteous words, you leave Baker Street, discouraged but eager to match wits with Mr. Holmes again. *Turn to 237.*

157

Now that you have finished testing the brandy, you help Holmes clean and put away the apparatus. As you scrub and wipe, he asks if there is any other help he might provide.

"I cannot leave Baker Street this morning," he adds, "but I will do all I can do from here."

•*If you ask about Colonel Sylvester, turn to 547.*
•*If you confront Hamilton, turn to 364.*
•*Otherwise, turn to 305.*

158

You carefully consider your next move.

•*If you checked Deduction 14, turn to 147.*
•*Otherwise, turn to 349.*

159

You recognize the bottled drug as something that could make a horse run more slowly, but it would have to be given to the animal several hours before the race to hamper his performance. *Check Deduction 9.*

•*If you checked Clue G, turn to 601.*
•*Otherwise, Turn to 302.*

160

"Evenin', guv," Stanly greets you. "I followed that man Oliver like you told me to."

•*If you checked Decision 21, turn to 123.*
•*If you checked Clue H, turn to 608.*
•*Otherwise, turn to 124.*

161

You gasp as the bullet hits you like a runaway train, then faint from pain.

You regain consciousness to find Watson tending your wound. As you try to rise, Watson stops you.

"We must get Hamilton," you mutter, still resisting him.

He shakes his head as he answers. "After he shot you, he stood up to get a better shot. I finished him instead. Now let me bandage you to a point where I can get you safely to the station. Then you must lodge with Holmes and me for a week or two, eh?" **The End**

162

As you mingle with the people near Phillips and the smith, Phillips notices you. "No, Bench," he says, looking around, "I think we'd better talk this over later, when we can be a little more private." With a nod of agreement, the two men separate. *Turn to 358.*

163

"What was your opinion of Colonel Sylvester?" you ask.

"Opinion," he almost snorts. "I come to this club because it is the one place in all of London where I can ignore everyone around me, and I am not forced to associate with them. I find the objects of my historical studies far more congenial than my contemporaries in the flesh." *Turn to 300.*

164

"There is a powder residue," you say after running the tests, "but there isn't enough to identify it."

"How unfortunate," Holmes mutters. "Was that all that was left in the glass?"

•*If you checked Clue K, turn to 385.*
•*Otherwise, turn to 373.*

165

You thank Lord Hampton for his time, stalling as you think of what loose end to pursue next. What timely task remains to be done, you ask yourself. *Turn to 212.*

166

Although you listen and watch with great care (under the pretext of mingling with the crowd), you are unable to learn anything of interest. *Turn to 668.*

167

"Saw, sir?" the waiter replies, a little puzzled. "Well, I didn't hardly see nothing. I just took the gentlemen their drinks. It was like it always is here at this club, all the men just sit and read and never say a thing. Most pleasant, I find it, not like some clubs where 'alf the members want to pretend they's your mate."

"How many drinks did Colonel Sylvester have?" you ask.

"The Colonel had two, sir. I remarked on it, for it was unusual for him. He generally just had the one glass while he was reading his paper." *Turn to 246.*

168

"We are nearing the end of the list," Sir Andrew says with a sigh of relief. "Will you see the Honourable Charles Martin, MP, or would you prefer to give him a miss?"

●*If you want to see Martin, **turn to 543**.*
●*Otherwise, **turn to 198**.*

169

"When we isolated the foreign material, you muttered something like 'Sunflight,' Mr. Holmes. What did you mean by that?" you ask.

"Oh? I talked aloud?" he asks, surprised. "Well, that is the common name for the chemical we found in the brandy. It comes from a West Indian plant; natives of those islands use it medicinally. Sunflight is a very powerful stimulant — hence the name. Physicians have discovered that it makes the heart beat much faster and elevates one's blood pressure. It is especially potent if the person ingesting it is already eager and excited."

Watson looks up, a look of understanding on his face. "Why, Holmes," he says, "given a man like Sylvester, who appeared to be a likely candidate for a stroke at any time, such a drug might well be lethal."

"Precisely," Holmes agrees. "A clever murder, and difficult to explain to a jury. The murderer's use of this drug helps us, though. Sunflight is very rare, only available in one or two of the smaller islands. The man who employed it must have some connection to the West Indies." *Turn to 157.*

170

"Why don't you like Irish Star, John?" you ask the doctor. "Mr. Holmes makes him sound like a perfect bet."

"Well," he answers, "what Holmes doesn't understand is that a horse doesn't always run true to form, and I have heard that Irish Star isn't going to run well today. And if you eliminate Irish Star, why, Maiwand is quite as good as any other horse in the race. Whatever Holmes thinks of me, I'm not fool enough to bet a bad horse just because I like his name." As Watson chuckles, Holmes remains aloof and unresponsive to his teasing. *Pick a number and add your Intuition bonus:*

●*If 2-7, **turn to 603**.*
●*If 8-12, **turn to 478**.*

171

You thank Colonel Stuart for answering your questions, and after a few words with Sir Andrew, he leaves. *Turn to 454.*

172

"I should like to search the stable, if I may," you tell the Colonel. "We may find some incriminating evidence."

The Colonel looks surprised, then nods. "Well, if you think it's necessary..." he says slowly. *Turn to 105.*

173

"Lord Hampton was responsible for the drugging," you state firmly. "He is the only suspect connected to the drug."

"A reasonable explanation," Holmes admits, "although it would have been wiser to prove that no one else had access to it. A motive would have been useful as well, but I think this evidence will do. Now, we must decide how to deal with his Lordship, who will be here in a few minutes."

•*If you want to try to solve the mystery again without being given the solution, turn to the Prologue and begin anew.*

•*Otherwise, turn to 185.*

174

You and Colonel Stuart have a small barn to yourselves; the only visible stall is Irish Star's. The barn appears old and worn, although there are signs that the owners of the track have been working to repair it. Colonel Stuart notices you studying it and laughs.

"It may not be the best barn here," he explains, "but they let me have it for nought as it is being repaired. We shall be here for a week only, and like my Scots ancestors, I'll save a penny wherever I can."

•*If you question Colonel Stuart, turn to 219.*
•*If you question his men, turn to 481.*

175

You consider your opinion that the mysterious note was a threat from Colonel Stuart to Colonel Sylvester.

•*If you ask Stuart about the note, turn to 476.*
•*Otherwise, turn to 350.*

176

"What utter nonsense," mutters Watson. *Turn to 999.*

177

"Well, anyone else?" Holmes asks, still smiling. "If not, you and Watson had better plan an itinerary for today's expedition."

"How about the solicitor, Hamilton?" Watson says. "He might be too obscure... "

•*If you ask about Hamilton, turn to 488.*
•*Otherwise, turn to 356.*

178

You realize that Lord Hampton is an ambitious man and wonder whether that ambition might include owning Irish Star.

●*If you ask Lord Hampton about offering to buy Irish Star,* **turn to 493.**

●*Otherwise,* **turn to 317.**

179

"Most racing people wager, sir," Raines agrees. "I'm one of the exceptions. I train horses for many men, and I get so much information that many of the best bets I could make would give me more trouble than the profits are worth. And more than that sir, I've been in this business for forty years, and I've seen all the ways a horse can lose. No horse is a sure enough thing to risk my money on. Just look at what happened to Irish Star today, and you see how risky any bet can be." **Turn to 380.**

180

You consider other questions for Sir Alexander.

●*If you ask his opinion of Colonel Sylvester,* **turn to 163.**

●*Otherwise,* **turn to 300.**

181

"I shall need to use your office, Sir Andrew," you say.

"Fine," he replies, perhaps wondering if you can stand up to the accomplished and tight-lipped members of the Club. *Check Decision 11. Turn to 189.*

182

Amber's Wine and Spirits is a small shop below a bigger business, with steps leading down from the street to its cavernous entrance. Inside it is dark and dusty, with shelves filled with hundreds of different bottles, most lying on their sides. The plump cheerful man behind the counter is obviously the proprietor.

"How may I serve you, gentlemen? The name is Amber," he eagerly volunteers.

"I am looking into the sudden death of Colonel Phillip Sylvester," you explain. "While there is little proof of foul play, I suspect as much. We understand that you furnished him with the St. Gabriel's brandy that he customarily drank?"

"Yes," he answers, considerably subdued. "Do you have reason to suspect that there was something amiss with the brandy from my shop?"

"Not at all," you answer quickly. "But the art of detection involves examination of every factor connected with a possible victim of foul play."

"Oh, I shall be happy to help then," Amber answers.

●*If you ask who supplied him with the brandy, **turn to 259**.*
●*Otherwise, **turn to 484**.*

183

The brandy from the bottle shows a very strong concentration of the drug, and it is easy to identify.

Watson looks very surprised and upset when he hears this. "But this widens the number of suspects, doesn't it, Holmes?" he suggests. "If the bottle rather than the glass was drugged, anyone could have done it. The guilty party need not have been at the club that night. However, I recall that Admiral Nelson saw Sylvester drink from the glass with no ill effect."

"No doubt, Watson. It is impossible to be certain, of course," Holmes reminds you. "Many things may have happened. To propound one theory, the killer may have slipped back to the bar after the vile act and dropped something into the bottle while others were distracted."

"Why would he do that, Holmes?" Watson demands. "Surely it would be a grave risk."

"He would think as you did, Watson, that such an action would broaden the range of suspects and thus protect him. If he had access to the brandy, he could be rid of all trace of the drug. With Colonel Sylvester dead, that would be a relief, I think."

After a pause, Holmes sighs and resumes his discourse. "There is this to be gained at least: this sample makes the identification of the drug certain." Then, half to himself he mutters "Sunflight," as though trying to remember something. *Check Clue R.*

"What was the drug, Holmes?" Watson asks.

"It is a West Indian drug called Sunflight by those who know it," Holmes answers. "It is almost unknown in this country, a very powerful stimulant. It could cause a man like Colonel Sylvester, a man susceptible to strokes in any case, to suffer one." *Turn to 157.*

184

You sniff the handkerchief and realize that it has been soaked in some kind of alcohol — perhaps the Colonel's brandy? Quickly you ask Watson for another glass jar and store the handkerchief in it. *Check Clue K. Turn to 207.*

185

The plans made, you are all seated and ready when Mrs. Hudson introduces Lord Hampton. The peer looks as dapper and distinguished as ever.

"Your invitation, Mr. Holmes, indicated that you would help to settle the matter of my purchase of Irish Star?" he asks eagerly. Then, noting the intensity of Holmes' look and the hatred in Colonel Stuart's eyes, he stops, his smile faded. "What is this?" he sputters. "Why are you looking at me like that? I demand that someone explain this inquisition!"

"I wonder," Holmes answers gently, "why a man of your reputation would see his name dragged in the mud, just to buy a horse more cheaply. You are wealthy, your Lordship; you could have paid more than the horse was worth and never noticed the loss. What will people say, I wonder? Will they ever let you on a track again? It's difficult to believe, but I have solid evidence now."

Lord Hampton does not deny the charge, or try to defend himself, instead turning so pale that you see Watson stir with professional concern. Then he bows his head in shame. "I do not deserve mercy," he sighs, "for it was greed that sealed my fate. I hated to see that great horse running so far below himself, when under my silks he would achieve fame. It is idle to say I would never repeat my crime — the stewards will warn me off for life, now." The man looks crushed.

Holmes' face softens a little. "Perhaps it is not too late," he answers. "I am not Scotland Yard. I suggest that you give orders to your solicitor that Colonel Stuart's stable be financed as it should. For yourself, I know that you have been offered a foreign appointment that would occupy you for the next two years. Purge your crimes by service to the Queen and with restitution to your victim. Thus, when Irish Star becomes a champion, you will have the satisfaction of knowing that you assisted him in his climb to excellence."

After a moment, the peer accepts Holmes' terms. He leaves with Colonel Stuart to arrange their financial agreement, and after a little more talk, you leave Holmes and Watson to walk back to your own quarters.

One question fills your mind: what will your next case be? *Turn to 237.*

186

You give Watson the note and ask him to lock it up at Baker Street. You decide to ask Holmes whether you should read it when you see him in the morning.

•*If you have checked Decision 20, turn to 189.*
•*Otherwise, turn to 203.*

187

You explain to Armand that you are looking into the death of Colonel Sylvester, and that you have heard that he dealt with the Colonel in the past.

•*If you ask his opinion of Colonel Sylester, turn to 243.*
•*Otherwise, turn to 412.*

188

You set out with Watson to continue the investigation. You start out walking, keeping half an eye for a cab.

"You know, cousin," you say, "I am pleased to have the opportunity to finish the matter out from under Mr. Holmes' eye. I appreciate all his help, but..."

"I know exactly what you mean," Watson laughs. "I treasure him more dearly than any other man I've known, but he is so confoundedly correct that he would make the most efficient man in the world doubtful of his wits. Who is first on our visiting list?"

•*If you checked Clue M, turn to 485.*
•*Otherwise, turn to 614.*

189

After arranging the chairs in Sir Andrew's office to suit yourself, you tell the Chairman of the Club that you are ready to begin interviewing witnesses. "You have been very thorough, Sir Andrew," you say, checking the list of names. "I should like you and Dr. Watson to remain in the room while I talk to the others."

"Very well," he says stiffly. "I hope that will minimize the trouble and inconvenience for all concerned. Sherlock Holmes suggested that his brother Mycroft should be interviewed first, if you are willing." You agree, and Sir Andrew sends a messenger to fetch Mycroft Holmes. It occurs to you that Sir Andrew would prefer a quiet investigation that fails to a successful investigation that brings undue publicity to the Diogenes Club. You wonder if he knows anything he hasn't told you yet.

•*If you ask Sir Andrew more questions,* **turn to 419.**
•*Otherwise,* **turn to 475.**

190

You realize that the two men collecting their winnings are Bowser and Fitzhugh, and find it interesting that the two notorious gamblers had bet so little. *Check Clue E. Turn to 527.*

191

"How could I be so stupid?" you say to yourself. *Turn to 999.*

192

Holmes listens carefully to your explanation, then nods. "Excellent!" he says. "You present a complete solution." *Turn to 546.*

193

Your test reveals absolutely nothing unusual in the brandy from the bottle. *Turn to 526.*

194

You and Watson decide to search the third building, a vacant tavern with a cellar. Watson enters the back door to search the upper level while you slip quietly into the basement.

You study the dark room for a moment. The former owners left many casks and crates around, providing good hiding places, but perhaps giving a cautious hunter a chance to sneak up on a foe. *Pick a number and add your Artifice bonus:*

•*If 2-7,* **turn to 284.**
•*If 8-12,* **turn to 127.**

195

"The only case that both Watson and I have faced that dealt with the racing world was that of Silver Blaze," Holmes continues. "And I am sure that Watson will make more from the story of that case than he will from his wagers." *Turn to 442.*

"And besides my horse's improvement, Mr. Holmes, the vet found evidence of the drug when he checked Irish Star the next day," Colonel Stuart adds. "He was given an experimental drug called 'HASTINGS DISTILLATE OF OPIUM.' Do you know of it, Mr. Holmes?"

The detective nods. "Of course I do. There was a paper written about it three or four years ago. That potion would certainly keep a horse from running well, at least if it were given him a few hours before the race. It could take a considerable period of time for it to act." *Turn to 335.*

•*If Decision 5 is checked,* **turn to 105.**
When you glanced over the stables, you had thought the groom customarily slept in the tackroom. Now you see that a wooden partition breaks the space into two little rooms. John Oliver's quarters consist of a shelf with his razor and combs, a cot with blankets folded on it, and a chest shoved under the cot. Clothes hang on three hooks on the wall. A small window with a sliding shutter provides a little air. *Check Decision 5. Pick a number and add your Artifice bonus:*

•*If 2-7,* **turn to 513.**
•*If 8-12,* **turn to 422.**

"The last name on the list. Thank God," Sir Andrew says, wiping his brow. "Admiral William Nelson. Will you see him?"

•*If you see the Admiral,* **turn to 509.**
•*Otherwise,* **turn to 596.**

"You know, Colonel," you begin, stopping him from sending for a constable. "We should have a difficult time proving a case against this villain. Why don't we just let him go? Mr. Raines can warn his colleagues, and we can rest assured Oliver will never get another chance to fix a race."

"You can be sure of that sir," Raines adds. "When I pass the word, he won't be able to do so much as get a job polishing the horses on a merry-go-round."

At first, Colonel Stuart resists the idea, but he finally agrees. Suddenly, Oliver climbs up and jumps out a window, escaping the uncomfortable scene. *Turn to 298.*

Looking at the label on the bottle, you recognize the "medicine" as a potion that would slow a horse. *Check Deduction 8. Turn to 126.*

201

"Was there any scandal attached to his service?" you ask. "Anything that could have led to today's tragedy?"

"Hardly," Sir Andrew answers stiffly. "Though it was rumored that he made some small mistake that led the commanders of our Indian forces to suggest that field command was not his forte. Also, it is nigh on fifteen years since he left — much too long for anyone to wait for revenge. The Colonel has been in business since his retirement." *Turn to 434.*

202

"Why were you so confident?" you ask. "I always thought trainers were aware of the many ways a horse can lose and thus never feel that confident before a race." *Pick a number and add your Communicationsbonus:*

• *If 2-5, turn to 290.*
• *If 6-12, turn to 242.*

203

You have finished your investigation at the Diogenes Club and feel confused and exhausted.

Watson seems to notice, commenting: "You look quite done up. Thinking is hard work, isn't it? You had best go home and rest. Remember, Holmes wants to see you at Baker Street in the morning. You must be ready, mentally and physically." *Turn to 627.*

204

A steward ushers in Mr. Henry Hamilton, who is introduced as a London solicitor. He is a solidly-built man, trim and fit apparently, although he coughs from time to time. You estimate him to be in his late thirties. From his clothes, he is successful although not wealthy.

"I appreciate your allowing me to ask you some questions," you begin. In certain ways, interrogating a solicitor makes you almost as nervous as questioning Holmes himself did. "Probably we will find that the Colonel died of natural causes, but it is well to be certain."

"I couldn't agree more," he answers pleasantly in a surprisingly high-pitched voice. "For a student of human nature, a few hours in the Diogenes Club is time well-spent, do you not agree? What may I tell you?"

• *If you ask about the note, turn to 102.*
• *Otherwise, turn to 420.*

"Did you think that I wrote this note?" he asks in surprise. You nod. "Why, I'm surprised at you," he says. "Still, I suppose it might make one suspicious. It would make me suspicious, though an heir seldom threatens the ruin of the man he will inherit a fortune from."

He glances at the note again, then smiles. "There is one other problem — my first name is Ian, not Henry. But perhaps you didn't know that?" You laugh together, and you're relieved that he is not angry. *Turn to 326.*

206

"But you said earlier that the Colonel was the kind of man who must receive warnings from time to time," you say pleasantly.

Hamilton blushes. "Well, I have heard about him, but that's not a relationship, you understand. I hear gossip as any man with ears and a brain does." *Turn to 537.*

207

"Do you want to look at the note Colonel Sylvester received this afternoon?" Sir Andrew asks, pointing to the victim's left hand. "It can hardly matter, I should think," he adds. "After all, Colonel Sylvester died before he could read it."

"Anything might matter, sir," Watson answers, and pries the note loose from the stiff fingers. "That's odd," he mutters, as he passes it to you.

You read the address before you react to his comment. The number 13 is written in the corner of the envelope, while its address reads:

Colonel A. J. Sylvester
At the Diogenes Club
Fleet Street, London

"What's odd, Doctor?" you ask.

"Why, that address," Watson answers. "We're on Pall Mall, not Fleet Street."

"Well, it hardly matters," Sir Andrew interrupts, "the note was delivered by hand. Now, if you want to talk to my bartender and other staff, I should appreciate it if you would do so now. Some of the members are growing impatient at the lack of service."

•*If you go to the bar,* **turn to 465.**
•*Otherwise,* **turn to 587.**

208

Feeling embarassed (and confident that Holmes would have told you anything of importance without questioning), you decide not to question the detective. *Turn to 133.*

"Lord Hampton is guilty," you say firmly. "He wanted to buy Irish Star, and its defeat would lower the price, due to Colonel Stuart's desperate financial position. And only Lord Hampton, of all the suspects, had access to the drug."

"Very good," Holmes replies, while Watson slaps you on the back in delight. "But," Holmes adds, "his Lordship himself will be here in a few minutes. How shall we command justice from the villain?" *Turn to 185.*

210

You and Watson take a cab and hurry to the address Holmes gave you. The hansom stops in a pleasant community on the outskirts of London. Hamilton lives on the upper floor of a small house.

You knock on the door and ask for the solicitor as Watson pays the driver.

"Mr. Hamilton?" the maid asks. "I shall see if he's willing to see you." She shows you into a back parlour and turns to go up to Hamilton's rooms.

"I think, ma'am," you say, "if you show him this note, he will be willing to see us." You hand her the coded message from Holmes.

You and Watson wait for barely a minute. Then you hear the landlady knock on his door, and, after a pause, a thud outside. Looking out the window, you see Hamilton running across the back yard. He jumps the fence and dashes into the alley.

Watson, gallant fellow that he is, is on his feet and running as quickly as you are. *Turn to 467.*

211

"I am afraid that Colonel Stuart committed the murder," you say. "He had motive, his need for money, and he might have learned of the drug when he served in the West Indies."

"He might," Holmes counters, "but I doubt that he did. Besides, with the odd terms of Sylvester's will, it was not in Stuart's interest to murder the Colonel. From everything I heard of his movements at the club, I doubt very strongly that he had the opportunity to drug the brandy." *Turn to 296.*

212

You pause to consider your next step. Whom shall I talk to next, you wonder.

•*If you checked Decision 4 , turn to 576.*
•*Otherwise, turn to 668.*

213

"We have established that Watson was distracted by the back page of the paper," summarizes Mr. Holmes. "So we must know what we always find on the back page. Many things may be there, but I know only one item that is listed there every day: the entries for the morrow's races. Now logically, if the thought of the race entries would distract Watson, he must have been writing about a case that dealt with races." *Turn to 195.*

214

With a crowd gathering outside the stables, a constable takes the shaken John Oliver away. *Check Decision 21. Turn to 336.*

215

"Did he tell you what the note said?" you ask.

"No. He handed me a sealed note and said only what I have told you.It appeared to me to have remained sealed at the moment the Colonel collapsed." *Pick a number* *and add your Intuition bonus:*

- *If 2-8, turn to 420.*
- *If 9-12, turn to 351.*

216

You shake your head in frustration. "I can't remember what's on the last page of the paper," you admit. "What distracted him, Mr. Holmes?" *Turn to 213.*

217

Light reflected from a medicine cabinet catches your eye; as the glare fades, you can clearly see the bottles inside. One reads: *HASTINGS DISTILLATE OF OPIUM.* You consider an immediate confrontation with Lord Hampton, then remember Holmes' instructions to act tactfully. Certainly a peer is a subject reqiring the greatest of tact. *Check Clue W. Turn to 165.*

218

Though there is no response to your knock, you hear a noise from inside that sounds like furniture being knocked about.

- *If you force the door, turn to 106.*
- *Otherwise, turn to 457.*

219

"I should like to ask you a few questions first," you say tentatively, "so that I can gain a good grasp of the situation before I interview the others."

"Whatever you think necessary," Colonel Stuart replies. "Just so we can solve this matter with all due haste."

- *If you ask about his employees, turn to 381.*
- *If you ask about Irish Star's defeat, turn to 103.*

"Opinion!" he says harshly, "why I shared the common opinion of all reasonable men who knew something of the man. Colonel Sylvester was a bastard of the first water. Even dead, he's troublesome." *Turn to 560.*

"Thank you for your time, Mr. Hamilton," you say politely. "I hope we have not wasted too much of your evening."

"My duty, I assure you," he answers, standing. In silence, Hamilton bows and leaves.

Watson catches your eye. "That man would be wise to find a more congenial climate," the doctor tells you. "That cough, and the slight pallor he showed, are not good signs." *Turn to 334.*

Holmes looks at you in astonishment and disgust as you name the party whom you believe drugged the horse. "No, no," he sighs. "I am grossly disappointed in you."

•*If you want to try again, turn to the Prologue and begin anew.*
•*Otherwise, turn to 148.*

"Did you know the man who gave you the note?" you ask Hamilton.

"No, I did not," he answers stiffly, eyes downcast, and then goes on when he looks up to see your look of disbelief. "He gave me a letter from a colleague of mine, stating that he was a reputable gentleman who needed a discreet service. As he offered a tidy sum in advance for my help and discretion, it did not seem wise to press him."

•*If you checked Decision 13, turn to 224.*
•*Otherwise, turn to 221.*

You ask Hamilton for a description of his employer. Stammering, the solicitor answers rather vaguely: "Well, I cannot be certain of much, for he was hidden in a great coat and broad hat. I gathered that a lack of curiosity was part of what he was paying for."

"Could he have been a foreigner?" you ask.

"I think not," he answers, pausing for a moment before adding: "However, he might have been — he did not have an obvious foreign accent, but there was something unusual...I would say just a little something in his word choice or phrasing was not entirely natural. He might have been foreign at that." *Turn to 221.*

225

A good distance from the clearing, you tell Watson: "Stay here, and I'll sneak up on him and jump him. To have any chance of success, he must not suspect that we are in the woods. Don't come unless I yell for you, or you hear him shoot."

Watson nods, though he obviously would like to do more himself. You begin to work through the woods, skirting the edge of the clearing. Then you drop down and crawl as you close in on Hamilton's hiding place. *Pick a number and add your Artifice bonus:*

●*If 2-7, turn to 330.*
●*If 8-12, turn to 672.*

226

You have your doubts when Hamilton denies all knowledge of Colonel Sylvester and seek the right way to question him further.

●*If you broach another line of questioning, turn to 411.*
●*If you accuse Hamilton of lying, pick a number and add your Communication bonus:*

  ●*If 2-8, turn to 345.*
  ●*If 9-12, turn to 580.*

227

You shake the dazed and fallen Oliver, then pour a bucket of water over him, just as Colonel Stuart and Raines run in.

"What happened?" the Colonel demands.

"When my questions got too close for comfort, Oliver came at me with his fists," you answer. "But he is no better at fighting than at lying." You shake the man again. "Now tell us the truth!"

"All right, guv, all right," the groom whines. "Just don't hit me no more. A man give me some stuff to put in the horse's water this morning. That's what made him run slow." Oliver cringes at the rage he sees in the faces of both Raines and Colonel Stuart.

"Well, let's get a constable to take care of this scum!" the Colonel growls. "Otherwise I might decide to horsewhip him myself!" Oliver flinches at the Colonel's threats. *Check Clue G.*

●*If you send for the police, turn to 214.*
●*Otherwise, turn to 466.*

228

Sensing that you have all the information you can gather, you stroll to the stables to talk to Colonel Stuart and his employees. A groom walking a horse tells you which barn to go to.

The Colonel greets you affably, although he is still obviously agitated.

"I hope you learned something," he says. "My men are waiting to talk to you." *Turn to 174.*

229

You show Colonel Stuart the note, explaining that it was delivered by a solicitor that evening. *Pick a number and add your Communication bonus:*

- *If 2-4, turn to 476.*
- *If 5-6, turn to 128.*
- *If 7-12, turn to 205.*

230

"Why did you come here today?" you ask. *Pick a number and add your Communication bonus:*

- *If 2-4, turn to 280.*
- *If 5-12, turn to 530.*

231

"Oh, please do," you reply, for the old seaman is obviously anxious to talk.

"Well, even in this silent place, all the rumour in the air is that someone poisoned Colonel Sylvester's brandy, and I know that isn't so."

Everyone in the room suddenly sits up. "How do you know, Admiral?" you ask softly.

"Why, it was this way," he continues, as if weaving a sea yarn. "I had just read a most upsetting piece in the Times and needed a drop to put my temper right. I buzzed, and saw the waiter come in, and I watched him with an eagle eye, you may be sure. He served Colonel Sylvester first. I could see my glass of grog on his tray, and I almost wanted to run over and grab it, I was so dry. So I fixed my eyes on the waiter and willed him to hurry over to me, but before he did, I saw the Colonel take a sip of the brandy. Now if it was poison, it would have killed him then and there, would it not?"

You can do nothing but nod.

"But once I got my grog," the Admiral goes on, "I returned to the Times and saw nought else until the Colonel fell down dead." *Check Clue O. Turn to 605.*

232

"What's this you're asking Bobby?" one of the jockey's friends asks. "You trying to say he done something to the stupid horse?" The ox of a man steps up to you with his fists raised.

To get any more information at the pub, you shall have to fight first. *Pick a number and add your Athletics bonus:*

- *If 2-6, turn to 261.*
- *If 7-12, turn to 304.*

233

"Did you notice anything while you were in the lounge today?" you ask, putting all possible respect into the words.

"In the lounge?" he repeats. "Why no, of course not. I am not supposed to see anything anywhere within the bounds of this club. Everyone clustering around so noisily when poor Colonel Sylvester fell down dead caught my eye, but I noticed nothing before that." *Turn to 550.*

234

"Why are you so opposed to my looking at your betting list?" you ask Roscoe.

"Well, Guv'nor, why should I let you look at me papers? Who are you, anyways, I'd like to know."

"I am trying to discover why Irish Star ran so poorly today," you answer. "You obviously expected it, for you laid off all the money on Maiwand and gave the best odds on Irish Star. Why?'"

"Oh, that," replies Roscoe, smiling sheepishly. "That's just a matter of business; nothing for no copper to worry about. I had word from a man who would know that Irish Star was off his form, so I set the odds accordingly."

"And you trusted the information?" you demand.

"I paid well for it," he answers, "and I'll pay more later. Everyone in racing knows better than to lie to me when there's that sort of money on the line." Roscoe anticipates your question, shaking his head as he speaks. "No, no, I won't tell you who it was. There's nought wrong with a businessman buying a little information, and I always promise to keep mum. And I will!" Roscoe's clerk helps the battered fellow walk toward the gate as Dr. Watson, calling out apologies, hurries to catch his train. *Turn to 228.*

235

You have broken the secret code! *Check Clue Q.*

•*If you are at the Diogenes Club,* **turn to 440.**
•*If you are at Baker Street,* **turn to 501.**

236

You take a deep breath, and Watson smiles as you point across the track. You walk slowly through the woods, walking carefully. You sigh in relief as the trees thin and you come up upon a little clearing.

Suddenly, you grab Watson's coat and pull him back among the thick trees. You catch a glipse of something on the other side of the clearing.

"Hamilton is waiting for us," you tell Watson. "He must have decided he must get rid of us to have any chance of escape."

Watson nods, whispering: "What shall we do about it?"

•*If you ask Watson to cover you while you rush Hamilton,* **turn to 250.**

•*If you tell Watson to wait while you sneak around and surprise Hamilton,* **turn to 225.**

Once you have a day or two to look back at it with some perspective, you carefully try to assess the lessons that you learned from investigating the Irish Star affair. You firmly resolve that when you get another chance to investigate, you will avoid the mistakes you made in analyzing clues and dealing with people.

One pleasant afternoon, you visit your cousin, Dr. Watson. He is alone in his lodgings and explains that Holmes has gone to his brother's club for the afternoon. You have a pleasant chat, reviving both your memories of a variety of family matters, a talk interrupted by a knock at the door. At a word from Watson, Mrs. Hudson enters and hands Watson a note. He reads it, and then his face puckers up thoughtfully. "Now how the deuce did he know?" he mutters.

"What did Mr. Holmes know?" you ask, aware that only one man can perplex Watson in that way.

"How did he know you would be here?" he answers, still a little distracted. "He asks me to bring you around to the Diogenes Club as quickly as possible." Watson stops and stares vacantly into space. "And how did you know the message was from Holmes?" he demands, but you are already helping him into his coat and handing him his hat.

"If Holmes wants you in a hurry — "

Fortunately, Watson quickly hails a cab. Your cousin's chatter is backgound music that only adds to your excitement. A case, and Holmes apparently wants your help!

To your even greater surprise, Inspector Lestrade of Scotland Yard is standing on the street outside the Diogenes Club when the cabbie drops you off. The policeman rebuffs Watson's cheery greeting with a snarl.

"I might have known you'd be popping 'round, Watson," he snaps. "You always do, any time that Mr. Holmes comes across anything the least bit mysterious."

"What has happened, Lestrade?" Watson demands. "We know nothing, except that Mr. Holmes ordered us to come here as quickly as possible."

"Happened!" the detective cries, and years of frustration add bitterness to his voice. "Cold-blooded murder, like as not, but they — " he sighs, tilting a shoulder towards the club, "don't wish the scandal of a police investigation. Colonel Philip Sydney Sylvester lies dead in there, struck down suddenly in the bloom of life. It may have been sudden illness, but they seem to think it poison. With the man's reputation, it might well be. But they refuse to let the police look into it, for they will not have the precious silence of their club disturbed by the bustle of a police investigation. And rot them, they have the influence to keep me from my job."

"But why did Holmes send for us?" Watson asks, breaking into the tirade.

8

"Holmes sent for you because he refuses to investigate the matter himself!" Lestrade shouts, quaking with frustration. "It's something to do with some promise he made at the time they elected him to membership. Holmes himself was in the room and is a witness to the death, making him a rather improper choice for investigator. So he sent for your cousin instead. Aye, I would love to be hidden in the walls and watch the great Mr. Sherlock Holmes stand silent while another detective questions and searches. I've had to do the same for him often enough myself. Well, good day and good luck to you gentlemen; you shall need it with that crowd."

When you ring you are immediately taken to the office of the Club's Chairman, Sir Andrew St. James. Sherlock Holmes sits in a corner, obviously unhappy at events, though he nods pleasantly enough to you and Watson.

"Thank you for coming so quickly," Sir Andrew begins. He is a well-dressed man in his fifties, elegant, and speaks with a slight lisp. "We have experienced a tragedy here today; there is talk of foul play. I felt the need to send for an investigator. Both the rules of the club and the nature of a good portion of our membership make it absolutely essential that the matter be considered with the utmost discretion and tact, at least until foul play can be established. You see, we customarily do not speak once we enter the Club — it is a refuge of silence."

Restraining your glee, you solemnly nod. At times, Watson has hinted that the Diogenes Club is a cover for some of the more secret branches of the government. This could be vitally important to the Crown!

"The facts are these," Sir Andrew continues. "Colonel Sylvester, one of our members, died very suddenly this afternoon. As he was in good health, there is some reason to suspect foul play. I have kept everyone here who might know anything, so that you may question those gentlemen whom you wish to interview. The body is still in the lounge where he collapsed, if you wish to look at it, although the ambulance attendants stand ready to remove it."

"I shall do my best," you quickly reply. "Can you tell me exactly how he died?'

"I shall try, without employing hearsay," Holmes says, interrupting St. James' reply. "Something upset the man, for he drained almost a full glass of brandy at a swig — the sort of brandy he normally would sip and savor. Almost immediately, he fell down dead. I regret that I cannot give the problem my own attention," he adds.

You nod. "Inspector Lestrade told us that the club rules prevented you from investigating," you add.

Holmes smiles his rare smile. "I wasn't fully truthful with Lestrade," he admits. "Tonight I must see a man who knows something of some missing jewels. If Lestrade knew his identity, he would feel bound to interfere and would probably delay the recovery of the missing property. Thus, I must leave soon, and there is much that must be done here tonight. That is why I sent for you. Do you wish to ask me any questions? I was in the room when the man died."

•*If you question Sherlock Holmes,* **turn to 433.**
•*Otherwise,* **turn to 208.**

238

You decide from the slightly stilted prose that some foreign enemy of Sylvester's sent the note. *Check Deduction 13. Turn to 648.*

239

You reread the strange note and try to comprehend its significance.

- *If you think a foreigner wrote it, **turn to 238**.*
- *If you think it has no connection to the murder, **turn to 648**.*
- *If you think it is written in code, **turn to 421**.*
- *If you think it was a threat from Colonel Stuart to Colonel Sylvester, **turn to 625**.*

240

"Which staff members served the Colonel today?" you ask. "That is, in a way that might have allowed them to see anything?"

"Only the waiter, Tom Smithson," he answers. "He brought Colonel Sylvester the glass of brandy which he drank just before he collapsed."

"Has he been in your employ long?" you ask.

"He's served here about six months," Sir Andrew answers. "Smithson is a quiet, lonely man — just what we like, because he's not inclined to gossip or disturb the members." *Pick a number and add your Intuition bonus:*

- *If 2-6, **turn to 119**.*
- *If 7-12, **turn to 657**.*

241

Though Hamilton fights desperately, you are too fast for him. A shrewd move trips him up, and as he struggles back to his feet, you put him to sleep with a tremendous uppercut to the jaw. Quickly you tie his hands and yell for Watson. *Turn to 613.*

242

"Usually, I would agree," Raines admits. "But Irish Star is a step above the horses he raced today. And not only was he better by far than the other beauties in the race, he also trained very, very well of late. Why, just two days ago I worked him with Lord Hampton's champion Queensland, and he ran stride for stride with him. Ask Lord Hampton if you want proof — he watched and he was mighty upset. 'Cause you see," Raines continues, as if lecturing a class, "on the racing form, Irish Star is a notch below the great stakes horses, just as he's a notch above the ones he raced today." *Check Clue D. Turn to 430.*

243

"I would be obliged," you continue, "if you would tell us what you thought of the late Colonel Sylvester."

Armand's face darkens; his eyes narrow with sudden hate. "Colonel Sylvester—I should be getting ready to dance on his grave, sir, but the man has ruined me again, by dying at the wrong time."

"How is that?" you ask.

"If you know anything, you know that Colonel Sylvester ruined me years ago. Very well, we live in a cruel world and deal in a difficult business. I understand that, Monsieur. But I also know that every dog has his day, Monsieur, and mine was coming. I make friends with the right government officials back home, and I have this Colonel Sylvester in the palm of my hand. He either give me back much of what he took away, or I ruin him. And what does he do? He goes and die. Bah!" *Turn to 412.*

244

"A penny for your thoughts," says Holmes. *Turn to 999.*

245

You nod at what Hamilton has told you, considering whether he might know anything else useful.

•*If you ask more about the Colonel, turn to 474.*
•*Otherwise, turn to 411.*

246

You ask Smithson about his background.

"Oh, I'm from London, sir; lived here and worked here all my life. Not like my brothers who joined the army, most of 'em. I been here at this club about a year, sir."

•*If you ask his opinion of Colonel Sylvester, turn to 671.*
•*Otherwise, turn to 269.*

247

After considering it for a few minutes, you conclude from the odd phrasing that the note was either written by a foreigner or that it is written in code.

•*If you think it is in code, turn to 421.*
•*If you think it was written by a foreigner, turn to 238.*

248

After studying the note further, you decide that it must have been written in code.

•*If you try to solve the code, turn to 421.*
•*If it is not worth the time, turn to 258.*

249

Your frantic dive misses Hamilton, and for a few seconds you lie stunned on the floor. When you regain your breath, you dash after him, yelling for Watson. *Turn to 567.*

"You still have your gun, don't you?" you ask.

"Certainly," he answers, pulling it out.

"Here is my plan, then. I will rush Hamilton and tackle him. You fire at him to make him keep low. Once I have him, you approach and he'll be forced to surrender."

"That's very dangerous," he starts to protest, but you wave him to silence.

"We don't dare give him time to get away again, now that we've found him."

Without a word you work your way to the edge of the trees and show Watson where you saw Hamilton. He settles into cover, checks his gun, and nods. Bending low and weaving back and forth, you charge across the clearing, shuddering as you hear the crack of Hamilton's gun. *Pick a number and add your Athletics bonus:*

- *If 2-4, turn to 389.*
- *If 5-7, turn to 161.*
- *If 8-12, turn to 153.*

251

"The cad!" exclaims Watson. *Turn to 999.*

252

"Did you wager on Irish Star, Mr. Raines?" you ask.

"No sir, I make it a point never to wager on the horses," the trainer frankly replies. "I feel it's not proper in my position."

- *If you rephrase the question, turn to 399.*
- *Otherwise, turn to 380.*

253

With a word from St. James, a steward leads you into a small lounge. Shelves full of leather-bound books line the walls. Around the room, comfortable chairs flank solid tables. In the corners and near the door, tables stand covered with the latest newspapers and magazines.

However, the colonel's body distracts you from further examination of the room. Colonel Sylvester was a large, heavyset man. He is stretched on his back on the carpet, arms outflung, his head turned to one side so that you can see his distorted face, made more ghastly by the bulging eyes and the mouth frozen into a ghastly grin. You hear Watson draw in his breath in shock. A glass lies by his hand on the carpet, while the other hand clutches an envelope. *Check Decision 20. Pick a number and add your Intuition bonus:*

- *If 2-6, turn to 152.*
- *If 7-12, turn to 492.*

"I think Roscoe paid Oliver to drug the horse," you say. "He has a most dubious reputation, and he did pay money to Oliver. His only reason to pay Oliver would be for fixing the race."

Holmes shakes his head. "I don't think we can blame him for this particular bit of misbehaviour," the detective reasons. "His moral code is certainly a most doubtful commodity, but this is not his cup of tea. I would say that Oliver sold Roscoe the information that Irish Star was not going to run well — your groom was entrepreneurial enough to ask for money from more than one source," Holmes explains to Colonel Stuart before continuing. "Yet Roscoe does not need to risk his business to insure the outcome of a race. A small edge is enough for a man of his ability. In addition, I doubt that he had access to the drug."

•*If you want to try to solve the mystery again without being given the solution,* **turn to the Prologue** *and begin anew.*

•*Otherwise,* **turn to 585.**

255

Reading the label on the medicine bottle, your realize that the drug would have slowed the horse and that it must have been given several hours before the race. *Check Deduction 9.   Turn to 126.*

256

You decide to fight Roscoe. Watson makes sure the clerk won't interfere but cannot give you any other assistance. *Pick a number and add your Athletics bonus:*

•*If 2-6,* **turn to 369.**
•*If 7-12* **turn to 545.**

257

You look at the note, think about it, and then decide that the note must be in code. Having made that decision, you decide to try the ciphers you know and quickly "break" the code. *Turn to 270.*

258

The coded note is amusing, but you decide that it likely has nothing to do with the murder, since Colonel Sylvester never had time to read it. You give the sheet to Watson for safekeeping and ponder what to do next.

•*If you checked Decision 20,* **turn to 189.**
•*Otherwise,* **turn to 203.**

259

"Who shipped the St. Gabriel's to you?" you ask.

Amber quickly replies: "I get it from a French shipper, Pierre Armand. He was once a major dealer, but now has only a limited business." *Check Clue S.   Turn to 484.*

"Mr. Holmes, did you see anything at the time that Colonel Sylvester died — whom he spoke with or what he did?"

Mycroft shakes his great head. "I am sorry to disappoint you, but I was deep in my reading of a report and did not look up until I heard the thud when he hit the floor. Of course, he talked to no one — such conduct is strictly forbidden in the Diogenes Club." *Turn to 130.*

Your last memory of the fight is a fist flying toward your face.

You wake up outside, with water rushing over your face and in your eyes. Another bucket revives you. Then the man who beat you and another oaf drag you to your feet and load you into a cab. "Take him to London," one of them orders the cabbie, handing him some money.

The man who beat you leans in and shakes a fist at you once more. "You just stay away from here!" he orders. "We catch you snooping around another time, it'll take two cabs to take your pieces back to London." With your temples throbbing, you hardly feel like arguing.

Surrendering the idea of meeting Holmes' irregular, you sit back in the cab, nursing a swollen eye and cut cheek. *Turn to 480.*

"Did you see any strangers near the stables this morning? Anyone who had no business being here?" you inquire.

Oliver thinks for a moment, squinting his beady eyes, then nods. "Yes, I did, guv, it so happens. I seen a couple gents named Bowser and Fitzhugh, what bets a lot. But then, them two hangs around the stables all the time, lookin' for a word to guide their wagerin', if you gets my drift. Course it would cost a man his job and a beating on top of it if he was to tip off a couple of touts like that." *Check Clue V. Turn to 309.*

You decide that Hamilton probably took the train west towards Bristol. From the time he fled his flat until he caught the cab, he hardly had the chance to conceive a more complex plan. You don't have to wait long before the Bristol Express pulls up at this station. You will actually be in that city before Hamilton's slower train reaches it.

You and Watson ride along, talking little, until you feel the train slowing down.

"We must be where the branch line for Market Blandings and the south coast leaves the main line," Watson mutters, stifling a yawn. "We must stop a few minutes to pick up passengers and mail."

A sudden thought strikes you. "I suppose you can get a south-bound train from here too?" you ask.

Watson nods in agreement. "I suppose so, though I don't know the schedule." Then his head jerks up. "Do you think Hamilton could have changed trains here?" he asks you. "Holmes used that trick to get away from Moriarty back in '91. But we don't have time to search for him, or we'll lose the train. It only stops here a couple of minutes."

You quickly consult the conductor, who tells you that no train has gone south from this station since the local passed through it. You ask if you could find out if anyone got out here, when the local came through.

"No sir, I doubt it," he explains. "Unless a man talked to the agent. At these small stations, the agent is too busy loading baggage and helping passengers on to pay attention to the ones getting off."

•*If you go on to Bristol, turn to 121.*
•*If you search this station for Hamilton, turn to 590.*

264

"Does that mean that the Colonel was not murdered?" Watson asks.

"What do you mean, Watson?" Holmes says.

"Why, the brandy from the bottle is untampered with, apparently, and the Admiral saw Sylvester sip from his glass with no ill effect. The brandy must have been all right, and that was the only possible method that might have been employed to murder him."

"A thoughtful analysis, Watson," Holmes says. "Do you agree with the Doctor?" he asks you.

•*If you agree, turn to 670.*
•*Otherwise, turn to 477.*

265

You cock an ear at Mycroft's words, recalling what St. James said. There was some disgrace in the Colonel's past.

•*If you ask Mycroft about Sylvester's past, turn to 656.*
•*Otherwise, turn to 632.*

266

"Fiddlesticks," says Mrs. Hudson. *Turn to 999.*

267

"Very good," Holmes says with a nod. "There is hope for you, I think. We shall have Lord Hampton here to rectify his misdeeds, although it will take a little tact, due to his rank." Holmes' slight compliments are music to your ears. *Turn to 185.*

268

"Is there anything you can tell me about Oliver that would help me in questioning him?" you ask. "The more a detective knows, the better prepared he is."

"What should I know about my groom? We hardly travel in the same social circles." The Colonel looks angry, then his expression changes. "There is one odd thing — before the race today, John passed by the wagering tables at the same time I did, and I overheard him place a bet on Irish Star. Surely he wouldn't have bet on the horse if he'd done anything to hurt him?" *Check Clue F. Turn to 481.*

269

You thank the waiter for his trouble.

"No trouble at all, sir," he answers and leaves. *Turn to 602.*

270

With rising excitement, you translate the note and read it to Watson and Sir Andrew. "It says," you explain: "'My life is pain from your disgrace. It cost me my love. The price — your immediate death. Henry Hamilton.'"

Hurriedly you consider the best action to take advantage of this information. *Check Clue Q.*

- *If you checked Decision 20, turn to 327.*
- *Otherwise, turn to 319.*

271

Remembering Holmes' constant emphasis on the need for patience, you continue to wait, watching the front of the buildings. Hamilton must come out eventually! Watson grows more and more restless by your side, and you signal him to calm down. *Pick a number and add your Observation bonus:*

- *If 2-7, turn to 573.*
- *If 8-12, turn to 313.*

272

"Did the horse train well for this race?" you ask. "I'd heard here and there that Star was on top of his form and ready to run."

"Well, sir," the groom answers, "I was thinking during the week that maybe this race was one too many before he had some time off, but who am I to judge? I just feeds him and mucks out his stall and such like." *Pick a number and add your Intuition bonus:*

- *If 2-8, turn to 641.*
- *If 9-12, turn to 515.*

273

"In a haberdashery?" queries Holmes. *Turn to 999.*

274

You decide that it would be wise to talk to Mr. Hamilton.

- *If you have Clue Q, turn to 607.*
- *Otherwise, turn to 204.*

275

"Did you know Colonel Sylvester personally, Admiral, or have any opinion of him as a man?" you ask.

The Admiral laughs, his whole great body shaking. "Know him! As little as I could, for the man was a coward and a blackguard. Fortunately, at this club I ignore all other members, a great comfort when they are men like him." *Turn to 622.*

276

Wondering if it will prove an important clue, you read the unopened note Colonel Sylvester held in his had at his death. *Check Decision 22.* The note is written on cheap white paper, probably copied by a hired clerk. The number 13 is written in the upper left corner. It reads:

My Dear Colonel:

Life for you is your wealth. Pain is yours from anyone attacking your riches. I shall disgrace you though it has the cost of ruining me as well. My heart will love to pay the world the price that produces your complete and immediate, permanent, financial death.

Lt. Col. Henry Stuart

Hotel Hamilton

You stop to consider the note. If it had not been sitting in a dead man's hand, would it have any significance, especially when the dead man never read it? *Pick a number and add your Scholarship bonus:*

- *If 2-5, turn to 239.*
- *If 6-7, turn to 247.*
- *If 8-9, turn to 248.*
- *If 10-12, turn to 257.*

277

"That's hardly cricket, eh what?" says Watson. *Turn to 999.*

278

Nothing comes immediately to mind when you study the note, considering it more carefully.

- *If you think it was written to implicate Stuart, turn to 639.*
- *If you think it was written by a foreigner, turn to 588.*
- *If you think it is written in code, turn to 308.*

279

After reading the note, your deduce from the stilted language that it was either written by a foreigner or written in code.

- *If you think a foreigner wrote it, turn to 588.*
- *If you think it is written in code, turn to 308.*

280

"I needed money desperately!" he snaps, his face red. "Why else? And the only chance I had was to plead with that rotter."

It obviously would do no good to ask him more. *Check Clue B. Turn to 171.*

281

You deduce that the note is written in code and resolve to "break" it. *You may reread passage 361.*

●*If you "break" the code, turn to 519.*
●*If you fail, turn to 315.*

282

"Mr. Smithson," you say kindly, "I know today's tragedy must have upset you, but could you tell us in your own words what you saw in the lounge today?" *Pick a number and add your Communication bonus:*

●*If 2-7, turn to 557.*
●*If 8-12, turn to 167.*

283

"What he was writing about?" you mutter. "Now what clues do I have?"

●*If you have checked Clue Z, turn to 383.*
●*Otherwise, turn to 424.*

284

Trying to move quietly as you search the celler of the abandoned pub, you bump a pile of boxes that fall and scatter, making enough noise to wake the dead. Hamilton leaps from his hiding place and dashes for a front door. You dive after him, trying to catch an ankle as he scrambles out. *Pick a number and add your Athletics bonus:*

●*If 2-8, turn to 249.*
●*If 9-12, turn to 612.*

285

"I say," you ask suddenly, "may I have a sample of that brandy of the Colonel's? It might help prove what happened to him."

The bartender hesitates a moment, then nods. He pulls out a cut-glass decanter and pours a finger of the liquid into another of Dr. Watson's jars. "It can't matter now," he laughs. "The Colonel certainly won't be drinking it any more." *Check Clue N. Turn to 122.*

286

"Without doubt!" Holmes snorts. "If you consider yourself a detective, it should be obvious to you that something was very wrong with Irish Star. Your question surprises and disappoints me. But it doesn't matter. It's good for Watson to score off me on occasion, and I have no time to look into the case before my train leaves." Holmes turns away, unwilling to go into any detail. *Turn to 654.*

287

You consider John Oliver's assertion that Irish Star had trained poorly for the race. Is he lying? *Pick a number and add your Intuition bonus:*

• *If 2-7, turn to 641.*
• *If 8-12, turn to 339.*

288

"What do you mean?" the valet demands. "Who are you to demand answers of me?"

"We shall call the police," you threaten idly.

The man's combative spirit collapses. "When I was young, Colonel Sylvester caught me in thieving when I needed money to save me father's life," he explains softly. "He's kept the papers, I am certain, and I came to destroy them before the law seizes them and the police come looking for me."

"Fine, fine," you say, trying to calm the man. "I understand your concern. But I must have some papers that might show something of how he carried out his business affairs, as to whether they reveal the identity of anyone who would want to kill him."

The valet actually laughs, a ghastly sound. "Sir, anyone who knew the bugger would want to kill him! But I'll find your papers. There's one file here that he kept specially safe."

You look through the special file. Most of the papers look like ordinary business correspondence, letters from employees of competing companies. All of them have the number 13 written in the upper left corner. From the text, you get a good idea of the kind of businessman Sylvester was — cunning, unscrupulous and mean.

• *If you checked Clue Q, turn to 518.*
• *Otherwise, turn to 505.*

289

As soon as you realize that the note is in code, you set out to "break" it. You test the codes you know and quickly find that you know the one the note is written in. *Turn to 297.*

290

"I'm one of the best in the country at training winning horses — I know when a horse is ready to win!" Raines insists, smashing a fist into his palm. "Ah, I told the Colonel it'd be a waste of time to talk to the likes of you. Good day." Angry, Raines walks away, leaving you in his wake. *Turn to 570.*

"I am investigating the death of Colonel Sylvester," you explain. "Mr. Hamilton has some connection with the case, and naturally his background may help to explain his part in the drama, if any."

The old man's face reddens and hardens with righteous indignation. "Connected with a murder! Nonsense! Nothing that Hamilton did with us years ago could have any such connection. Jones, show these gentlemen out."

The clerk shows you to the door with little ceremony, and you and Watson must contemplate your next step. *Turn to 158.*

292

"What are you about, sir?" you demand.

The valet looks up angrily.

"Come sir, we wish you no harm," you assure him. "We only want evidence in the Colonel's death." *Pick a number and add your Communication bonus:*

- *If 2-5, turn to 637.*
- *If 6-12, turn to 288.*

293

Your conversation brings you to Roscoe's booth, just as a very distinguished-looking man comes up. Roscoe hurries behind the table to deal with him personally, accepting a ticket and handing over a handful of money.

"There you are, Lord Hampton," says Roscoe, grinning nervously, "five pounds at eight to one will give you forty-five pounds back. Surprised you didn't back him more heavily, him being your own nag."

Lord Hampton stuffs the money in his pocket, chuckling. "Don't tell my people, Roscoe," he almost whispers, "but I didn't have much faith in my horse. Just two days ago, Irish Star ran against my champion, Queensland, in a workout and matched him stride for stride. Since Queensland is much faster than Maiwand, I didn't think he had a chance, so I just bet a little for form's sake. If I'd known Irish Star was so off his feed, I'd have bet my all." Tipping his hat, Lord Hampton strides gracefully away. *Check Clue D.*

You notice two men collecting eighteen pounds from the clerk, while Roscoe is paying off Dr. Watson. *Pick a number and add your Observation bonus:*

- *If 2-5, turn to 527.*
- *If 6-12, turn to 190.*

294

After correcting your mistake, Holmes lights his pipe and settles back to explain the case. "The evidence points to John Oliver,

Colonel Stuart's groom, as the man who drugged Irish Star. He certainly would have had access to the horse at the right time for the drug to work, a fact that is true of few others. Oliver also predicted that Irish Star would run badly when everyone else around the track expected him to run well, and a groom, especially a poorly-paid one, would be an easy target for a generous bribe."

Colonel Stuart blushes at the mention of his financial woes. *Turn to 460.*

295

"No, I think I had better not read the note," you decide. "The matter is confusing enough without examining extraneous factors."

"Perhaps I should lock it up for safekeeping," Holmes suggests, and you hand him the note. He opens it and reads it first, but says nothing. You and Watson know better than to question Holmes at such times. *Turn to 405.*

296

You have failed to solve the murder of Colonel Sylvester correctly.

●*If you want to try to solve the case again, turn to 237.*
●*If you want to hear Holmes' explanation of the murder, turn to 520.*

297

With your heart beating faster from the excitement, you read aloud the translation to Holmes and Watson.

"The note was in code," you exclaim. "It reads thus: 'My life is pain from your disgrace. It cost me my love. The price, your immediate death. Henry Hamilton.' Hamilton, the man who brought Colonel Sylvester the note!" *Check Clue Q. Turn to 501.*

298

Certain that you have learned everything possible at Colonel Stuart's stable, you decide to leave. Bidding the Colonel a good day, you remind him that you will continue your investigative efforts elsewhere.

Walking back towards the track, you see a group of high-spirited men congratulating a slender, well-dressed fellow. As you get closer, and the men shout of how well his horse ran, you realize that this richly-appointed man is Lord Hampton.

●*If you talk to Lord Hampton, turn to 583.*
●*Otherwise, turn to 212.*

299

"Could the writer have been a foreigner?" you ask, feigning a tone of sudden inspiration. "You met the man who presumably wrote it."

Hamilton looks stunned at the question, then stops to think. "Yes," he says, "you may well be right. Perhaps a German or Swede, well-educated in English. When he spoke, I noticed the effort he made to speak without an accent, rather than any particular accent itself. He seemed to speak a little too precisely, as though he had to think how the words sounded in English. And one sees the same sort of effort in the note."

You nod, as if agreeing.

● *If you ask about a business competitor,* **turn to 633.**
● *Otherwise,* **turn to 401.**

300

Sir Alexander is obviously restless. With no more questions to ask, you quickly thank him and rise to hold the door for him. **Turn to 461.**

301

Your test reveals nothing unusual in the brandy from the bottle. **Turn to 526.**

302

You carefully put the bottle in your jacket pocket and wonder whether you should search other parts of the stable.

● *If you search further,* **turn to 105.**
● *Otherwise,* **turn to 298.**

303

What shall I ask Lord Trent, you wonder.

● *If you ask Trent his opinion of Sylvester,* **turn to 568.**
● *Otherwise,* **turn to 560.**

304

You knock down the jockey's heavy friend with a right cross and turn to face the little rider again.

"Well, mate," he says slowly, eyeing his fallen friend. "I guess you earned an answer to your question." **Turn to 138.**

305

"There is so much that would be useful to know," you sigh, "but I fear wasting your time asking about men who probably don't matter."

"Don't let that worry you," Holmes says. "The only way you will learn to differentiate the wheat from the chaff is by practice."

● *If you ask about Colonel Stuart,* **turn to 516.**
● *If not,* **turn to 413.**

"You say only a few men tested it?" you ask, and the vet nods. "Do you remember who they were?"

"I don't recall all the names," the drunken veterinarian explains. "I believe most of them were Scots or Irish. Dr. Hastings was a Scot himself and tended to people from his own part of the country. The only one who runs horses down here was Lord Hampton." You bid the man a good evening. *Check Clue X. Turn to 480.*

307

"Well, guv," Stanly says slowly, talking between bites of a piece of bread he grabbed off your plate. "I followed Bowser and Fitzhugh, just like you told me, but they didn't do nothing interesting at all. Didn't collect big from anyone nor talk to anyone more than hello-goodbye talk. When they got a cab to go back to London, I come over here to report, such as it is." You thank Stanly for his help and leave the smoky, crowded pub. *Turn to 129.*

308

Thinking that the letter may be in code, you decide to reread it. **Turn to 281.**

309

Satisfied that you have gotten all the information possible from John Oliver, you dismiss him. The groom takes a bucket and goes out after water.

As Colonel Stuart has calmed down, Henry Raines, the trainer, is now willing to talk to you. Up close, the man shows the quiet self-confidence typical of the true professional.

•*If you have Clue G, turn to 336.*
•*Otherwise, turn to 353.*

310

"What sort of men are they?" Colonel Stuart repeats. "They're obviously honest, hard-working men — I wouldn't employ any other sort. If I had cause to doubt either man, I shouldn't have had to seek out some foolish detective to help me. I would simply have called Scotland Yard!" *Turn to 481.*

311

Holmes continues to guide your analysis of the scene. "Now, the next question to address is: was Watson writing letters or one of his stories? Try to tell just by looking at his desk — it should provide all the clues you need." *Pick a number and add your Observation bonus.*

•*If 2-6, turn to 574.*
•*If 7-12, turn to 110.*

312

"Well," Holmes says, "Are you ready?"

You nod.

"First tell us who actually drugged Irish Star," Holmes adds, "then we can proceed to the matter of who ordered the act."

- *If you name the jockey,* **turn to 222.**
- *If you name Raines, the trainer,* **turn to 579.**
- *If you name John Oliver, the groom,* **turn to 354.**
- *If you name Bowser and Fitzhugh,* **turn to 145.**

313

In spite of Watson's restlessness, you concentrate on the three buildings, sweeping your eyes back and forth from one to the other. You are rewarded when Hamilton emerges, dashing across the street, calling for a cab.

You run to intercept him, and as he tries to sidestep, you dive for his legs. ***Pick a number*** *and add your Athletics bonus:*

- *If 2-6,* **turn to 249.**
- *If 7-12,* **turn to 141.**

314

Hamilton fights desperately against you, but he cannot match your agility. A hip toss stuns him, and as he struggles to his feet, you lay him out with a murderous uppercut to the jaw. After binding him, you call for Watson. **Turn to 613.**

315

"I cannot break the code," you admit, disgusted.

"I rarely have any luck with such things either," Watson says kindly. "Sometimes I think Holmes claims to find meanings when they are not really there, just to torment us lesser mortals." ***Turn to 584.***

316

The code is more obtuse than you can bear. ***Turn to 438.***

317

"I don't go to the races often," you say, "but it seemed to me that Irish Star looked sluggish when he came onto the track. I'm surprised the Stewards let him run."

"Oh, the Stewards would be very reluctant to scratch him," Lord Hampton brusquely replies, "especially considering the popularity of the horse."

- *If you checked Clue H,* **turn to 662.**
- *Otherwise,* **turn to 165.**

318

"Fiendishly clever," says Holmes. ***Turn to 999.***

After you explain the note, Sir Andrew sends for Mycroft Holmes. You tell Mycroft what the coded message means, and he nods in appreciation of its importance.

"Still," he adds, "I would not rush the matter. The man is no longer here, and he cannot guess what we have learned. Consider the best way to deal with him, and then discuss it with Sherlock when you visit him in the morning."

You get little sleep that night, pondering the clues, but you manage to keep your eagerness under sufficient control to avoid arriving at 221-B until after breakfast.

Holmes and Watson greet you warmly, and the three of you consider the import of the decoded note. *Turn to 501.*

320

"Why did you tell your brother Irish Star would lose?" you ask.

The groom recoils from the question, as if struck a blow. *Pick a number and add your Communication bonus:*

- *If 2-7, turn to 649.*
- *If 8-12, turn to 616.*

321

"I'm a little surprised to see you throwing such a party on a night that you lost so badly," you say, trying to think of something better to keep the conversation going.

"And I'm surprised you think that's any business of yours," the jockey snaps. "I rode three winners today, and that's good cause for a party. Besides, I might as well spend my money on my mates — there's nothing else to spend it on when you got to keep in shape to race every day of the season." Without another word he turns his back and calls for another round for his friends. Obviously, the jockey wants nothing more to do with you. *Turn to 439.*

322

"In for a penny, in for a pound," says Holmes. *Turn to 999.*

323

"I am sorry, Mr. Holmes, but I cannot guess why he didn't read it. Even if I were preoccupied with something, I would read the telegram because it might bear on what was worrying me."

"No, no!" Holmes replies, "Use your head! You had something when you said that Watson was preoccupied with his writing. When Watson takes up his pen, he keeps at his work for a good stretch." *Turn to 311.*

324

"Lord Hampton is the guilty party," you boldly assert. "He wanted to buy Irish Star, and a poor performance would lower the price."

"An unpleasant plot, indeed," says Holmes. "You are correct in your conclusion, but your case would appear stronger if you had connected his lordship to the drug. However, he will be here in a few minutes, and we must agree upon a course of action."

●*If you want to try to solve the mystery again without being given the solution,* **turn to the Prologue** *and begin anew.*

●*Otherwise,* **turn to 185.**

325

"To my mind, the outcome was arranged by Bowser and Fitzhugh, the gamblers," you say. "They probably went by the stables that day to be certain that Oliver had done the job."

Holmes shakes his head. "No, though I would be pleased if it were. But those two cads did not wager enough to indicate such an act. I have checked certain sources and found no evidence of their earning a great deal of money on any account. And with those two, no profit means no motive, and no case."

●*If you want to try to solve the mystery again without being given the solution,* **turn to the Prologue** *and begin anew.*

●*Otherwise,* **turn to 585.**

326

"I am afraid I know little of your cousin," you say.

"Lucky man," Stuart mutters.

●*If you ask him about Sylvester,* **turn to 471.**

●*Otherwise,* **turn to 659.**

327

You explain the code to Sir Andrew and Dr. Watson. They agree that it certainly casts the strongest suspicion on Henry Hamilton, especially as he is the man who delivered it to Colonel Sylvester. You agree that you should have him return to discuss the case, and then find a way to spring the trap and get a confession from him.

"But I think," Sir Andrew adds, "that you would be wise to have Mycroft Holmes here while you talk to Hamilton. He may make the difference in getting the answers you require. Also, if the man confesses, an extra witness will do no harm."

You agree, and Sir Andrew sends a messenger for Mycroft Holmes. You begin to wonder whether the Club's director has told you everything he knows.

●*If you question Sir Andrew,* **turn to 419.**

●*Otherwise,* **turn to 475.**

328

Hamilton's heavy boots shatter the frame, and as his body crashes thorough, he grabs the upper sash just enough to slow his momentum.

Running to the window, you see him land on his feet, roll forward and, back on his feet, scramble toward a waiting hansom. Before you can draw breath to shout for help, the driver whips his horse and the cab disappears around the corner.

Dr. Watson stops you as you turn to run for the room's door.

"Easy, my friend," he says slowly, "more thought and less leg."

"But he'll escape!" you cry.

"No, he must go to his rooms — however poised to flee, he must have left at least a bag there. Let's give chase." Sir Andrew hands you Hamilton's card, which has his home address written below the name. *Turn to 364.*

329

Your quick tackle brings Hamilton down, and though he tries to punch free, you have no trouble holding him, for Watson and Sir Andrew all quickly help. In a matter of forty-five minutes, Inspector Lestrade appears to take him away.

Your ensuing visit to Baker Street turns to a discussion of the case. *Turn to 331.*

330

You were not quiet enough as you moved through the woods. Hamilton hears you, spins around and fires a shot that hits the tree beside you. As you leap for the killer, he fires again. *Pick a number and add your Athletics bonus:*

- If 2-4, turn to 389.
- If 5-7, turn to 161.
- If 8-12, turn to 153.

331

"A sad case, Holmes," Watson comments. "If the man were not so bitter, you might sympathize with him."

"Perhaps, Watson," the detective answers drily, "though I have found that all but the most common criminals have a way of finding reasons to hide the true motive of their misdeeds. Still, even with his confession, it will be difficult to convict Hamilton of more than manslaughter. A clever barrister might sway a jury to the degree that Hamilton may go free. Who can say? It will also be difficult to prove that the chemical, whatever it was, actually caused Colonel Sylvester to die of a stroke."

"Well, Holmes," Watson counters, "at least no others stand under any charge in the matter. We never can be sure of what will happen once the man is handed over to the law. And your joy is ever in the chase, not its aftermath."

"Perhaps, Watson, perhaps," the detective mutters.

You share Holmes' feelings — now that this case has been brought to a successful close, you are already wondering what your next test might be. **The End**

You explain that you think Oliver drugged the horse because he bet on him; Holmes' eyes widen with astonishment. "With no other evidence, betting on a horse hardly seems proof that the man drugged him — even though you have managed to hit upon the correct name. But even Watson guesses correctly upon occasion."

•*If you want to try to solve the mystery again without being given the solution,* **turn to the Prologue** *and begin anew.*

•*Otherwise,* **turn to 294.**

333

Once again you ask Hamilton what he thought of Colonel Sylvester. *Pick a number* *and add your Communication bonus:*

•*If 2-6,* **turn to 337.**

•*If 7-12,* **turn to 342.**

334

Sir Andrew again consults his list. "The next man you should talk to is Colonel Stuart," he says. "He is the only non-member remaining and did not see Colonel Sylvester until he came in to view the corpse."

•*If you interview Colonel Stuart,* **turn to 403.**

•*Otherwise,* **turn to 454.**

335

"Now, young man," Holmes says, turning to you, "suppose you tell us just how this deed came to happen, and who is responsible."

You first detail the evidence you found and then summarize what happened in the course of your investigation. You try not to talk too much, fearing the embarrassment of presenting Holmes a faulty solution.

•*If you have checked Clue G,* **turn to 522.**

•*Otherwise,* **turn to 443.**

336

"Mr. Raines," you begin, searching for the right words, "do you have any idea of why Oliver would have drugged the horse?"

"For money, of course," Raines snaps. "Someone must have promised him a good fee to do the dirty job. And if I knew who, I'd hunt them out and break their ruddy necks. Makes me look bad, to lose when I was certain sure I had the race in my hand."

•*If you ask why he was so confident,* **turn to 202.**

•*Otherwise,* **turn to 430.**

337

"I already told you I didn't know Colonel Sylvester!" Hamilton says sharply. "I don't see why I should waste more time talking to someone who doesn't listen to my answers." He shifts in his chair, preparing to stand and leave.

•*If you let him go,* **turn to 387.**
•*If you ask why he wrote the note,* **turn to 417.**

338

"I think he's writing letters," you say slowly. "Probably a batch of letters telling a number of colleagues about some matter. He is anxious to get them all done, and therefore ignores everything else."

Holmes looks disappointed at the answer. "At least you don't parrot me," he says. "When I analyzed Watson's actions, I said he was writing a story. But aside from that, look closely. If a man writes a number of letters, does he pile the finished letters at his side, or does he put one in an envelope and stamp it before he writes the next one? In addition, wouldn't Watson have some address book handy if he were writing to a number of people?"

You nod slowly, agreeing with Mr. Holmes' logic. "Now look closely at the crumpled papers at his feet. If he were writing to a number of the people on the same matter, would he so foul some sheets that he just crumples them and throws them aside? No, that is the sign of the creative artist, frustrated when his thoughts take some false turn. Now see if you can tell what story Watson is writing."
Turn to 283.

339

"Don't try to make me believe a story like that," you tell Oliver, speaking sharply. "I'm no fool. Now have the courage to tell me the truth or you may face sharper questioning at Scotland Yard!" ***Pick a number*** *and add your Communication bonus:*

•*If 2-9,* **turn to 346.**
•*If 10-12,* **turn to 524.**

340

"I'm sorry, guv, but by the time I got this bottle he threw away, he'd gotten away, and I didn't lay an eye on him again until he come back to the stable." *Turn to 129.*

341

"Amazing!" exclaims Watson. *Turn to 999.*

342

Hamilton looks angry when you repeat the question, then shrugs. "I would rather not admit that I knew someone like the Colonel," he says slowly, "but I suppose that I have no choice in the matter. I have met him a time or two, and I learned a little about him before I accepted the assignment to bring him the message. An unscrupulous, nasty man, I should say. I had no desire to know him better."

•*If you decide to let him go,* **turn to 387.**
•*If you ask him why he wrote the note,* **turn to 417.**

343

As you raise the glass, you notice that the Colonel's handkerchief, clutched in his right hand, is soaked with some kind of liquid. Curious, you sniff at it, trying to identify it. **Pick a number** *and add your Scholarship bonus:*

• *If 2-5,* **turn to 441.**
• *If 6-12,* **turn to 184.**

344

"What sort of man was Colonel Sylvester?" you ask. "I've never heard of him."

"That's hardly surprising," he answers, an odd smile on his face. "With the Colonel, anyone who knew of his career tried to forget it as quickly as possible. In the army, he gained his rank in India, assisted by his wealth. However, he found campaigning not to his taste and retired to apply himself to mercantile endeavors here in London."

• *If you ask about Sylvester's military service,* **turn to 201.**
• *Otherwise,* **turn to 434.**

345

"That hardly sounds likely," you say.

The Solicitor's face turns very red, and his fists clench. Then he rises. "I can hardly see the relevance of a note the Colonel did not open to an investigation of a death that was probably natural, but I certainly see no reason to waste my time when you do not believe what I say. Good evening, gentlemen," he says, nodding to the Dr. Watson and Sir Andrew but pointedly ignoring you. He seems flustered as walks out.

"That was ill-spoken," Watson counsels."Let us hope for your sake that he is as unimportant as he seems." **Turn to 334.**

346

"What d'you mean, tell you the truth?" Oliver demands, flushing with anger. "I never lie to no man, and I don't have to stand for no man calling me no liar, neither." **Turn to 641.**

347

As Roscoe and his clerk attend to the fallen Dr. Watson, you quickly scan the list of bets. To your surprise, no one bet more than five pounds on Maiwand at Roscoe's booth; your quick glance reveals no heavy bets on any of the other long shots. You straighten up as Watson gets shakily to his feet. "Are you all right, Doctor?" you ask with feigned anxiety.

"I am, cousin, but no thanks to you," he answers gruffly. "It's safer chasing murderers with Holmes. I must run or I'll miss the train," he adds, and hurries off. **Turn to 228.**

348

"What a ridiculous idea," says Holmes. *Turn to 999.*

349

"We have one more visit, cousin," you tell Watson. "Mr. Holmes was very definite that I visit Colonel Sylvester's flat, to see if I can find any material bearing on his death or affairs. I may need your help if his staff is uncooperative." *Turn to 458.*

350

"You were Colonel Sylvester's only relation and heir?"
Colonel Stuart nods. "I did not choose him."

•*If you ask about his relationship to Sylvester, turn to 392.*
•*Otherwise, turn to 462.*

351

Something in his reply makes you uneasy — perhaps his mention of a warning.

•*If you press Hamilton for more information, turn to 345.*
•*Otherwise, turn to 420.*

352

You recognize the name of the drug on the bottle and realize that the drug could well make a horse run more slowly. *Check Deduction 8.*

•*If you have Clue G, turn to 601.*
•*Otherwise, Turn to 302.*

353

You search for just the right question to ask Raines.

•*If you ask him if he bet on Irish Star, turn to 252.*
•*If you ask him why the horse ran badly, turn to 453.*

354

Holmes smiles one of his rare, thin smiles. "Very good," he says, "you have indeed named the guilty man." *Turn to 621.*

355

Throughout your questioning, Martin consults his watch repeatedly. Taking the hint, you thank him for his time and bid him a good evening. *Turn to 198.*

356

Finished checking suspects' records in Holmes' files, you begin to plan an itinerary for the day's business. As you and Holmes prepare the list, Watson surprisingly interrupts you.

"I say," he begins, "I just remembered I might have something that could be of help, up in my trunks."

•*If you accept Watson's offer, turn to 388.*
•*Otherwise, turn to 426.*

357

"I did read the note, Mr. Holmes," you tell him. "Dr. Watson has it in his keeping."

As Holmes waits, Dr. Watson passes him the note. The detective quickly reads it, nodding as he does so.

"Well, what did you make of it?" Holmes finally asks.

•*If you checked Clue Q and Decision 20, turn to 359.*
•*If you checked Clue Q but not decision 20, turn to 370.*
•*If you checked Decision 12, turn to 494.*
•*If you checked Decision 13, turn to 372.*
•*Otherwise, turn to 447.*

358

Holmes and Watson return from placing their bets, continuing their earlier argument about the horses. As they settle comfortably on the grass, trumpets sound for the horses to enter the track, and outriders lead the thoroughbreds onto the track.

Dr. Watson rises eagerly. "There they come, Holmes," he says, pointing at the horses. "Irish Star is the handsome gray under the yellow and blue silks. Maiwand is the black: his rider wears brown. Do you see them?" *Pick a number and add your Observation bonus:*

•*If 2-7, turn to 508.*
•*If 8-12, turn to 651.*

359

"The note was written in code, Mr. Holmes," you explain, "and when I decoded it, I found that Henry Hamilton, the solicitor who carried it to the club, composed it as a death threat to the Colonel. However, I decided it would be better to gather more evidence before I confronted him."

Holmes nods encouragingly. "Well done," he says. "At the current stage of your career, it is probably just as well to be cautious about these things. Let us get on with the work, then." *Turn to 405.*

360

"I think the jockey did it," you say, "when he slipped something to the horse just before the race."

Holmes looks astonished. "How could you bring such a charge?" he asks. "Or think such a thing? With the drug that was used, the horse must have been doped long before the jockey ever touched him. Irish Star was already showing the lethargy from it when he approached the starting line."

•*If you want to try to solve the mystery again without being given the solution, **turn to the Prologue** and begin anew.*

•*Otherwise, **turn to 294.***

361

You open the envelope and look at the note. The number 13 is written in the upper left corner. It is written on cheap paper and appears to have been copied by a professional clerk. It reads:

My Dear Colonel,

Life for you is your wealth. Pain is yours from anyone attacking your riches. I 'll disgrace you though it has the cost of ruining me as well. My heart will love to pay the world the price that produces your complete and immediate, permanent, financial death.

Lt. Col. Henry Stuart

Hotel Hamilton

After reading the note once, you look up, puzzled. "It certainly is odd," you comment. It takes no urging for you to let the others read it. After a few minutes' thought, Watson voices his opinion in the matter.

"I see two possibilities," he says, "although I don't know that either would apply to this case. From the stilted language, a foreign enemy of Colonel Sylvester might have written it. Since Colonel Stuart is too poor to insult his possible benefactor so fiercely, it is possible that some enemy of his wrote it to try and destroy relations between the two Colonels. But in either event, I fail to see how it could effect your case." He too shakes his head in a puzzled way.

"What do you make of it, Mr. Holmes?" you ask.

Holmes shakes his head, addressing you: "It is your investigation, and I would rather not prejudice it with my opinion until you give the case up or fail. But perhaps I should listen to your opinion. You are the detective, but I might be able to find some mistake in your logic. First, reread the note: take your time." *Pick a number and add your Scholarship bonus:*

•*If 2-5, **turn to 278.***
•*If 6-7, **turn to 279.***
•*If 8-9, **turn to 281.***
•*If 10-12, **turn to 289.***

362

"Why do you think Irish Star ran so badly?" you ask.

Lord Hampton takes his time before answering. "It certainly surprised me," he says slowly. "The horse trained with my best earlier this week and all but beat him. Irish Star should have finished lengths ahead of Maiwand and the rest. But that's racing," he adds, changing his tone slightly. "You can never be sure what a horse will do, no matter how good it is." *Check Clue D. Turn to 629.*

363

Watson looks at his watch. "Come along, Holmes," he urges, "let's place our wagers before the horses for the main event are brought out. There's no sense waiting when we know which horse we want to back." The two men walk toward the wagering tables, leaving you unattended.

Awaiting their return, you overhear two men talking behind you mention "Irish Star," causing you to look at them. One is Phillips, the grain dealer Holmes pointed out to you earlier. From his massive size and leather apron, the other man appears to be a smith. Phillips is doing the talking. You decide to try and sneak close to them and overhear their conversation. *Pick a number and add your Artifice bonus:*

• *If 2-5, turn to 162.*
• *If 6-12, turn to 538.*

364

You and Watson take a hansom from the Diogenes Club and hurry to Hamilton's address. As you pull up outside a small house on the outskirts of London, you see your quarry flee across the backyard and jump the fence into the alley beyond.

You and Watson race after him, the driver calling out for his fee. *Turn to 467.*

365

"A capital idea," says Watson. *Turn to 999.*

366

"There were six club members in this lounge when the Colonel died," you say. "Did any of them have any particular connection to or knowledge of him?"

Sir Andrew frowns for a moment. "Did they indeed?" he grimaces. "Colonel Sylvester was not a well-loved man. He had strongly opposed admitting Sherlock Holmes to the club, claiming in notes to the membership committee that his membership could provide a cover for Mr. Holmes' detecting activities. Both Sherlock and Mycroft Holmes resented that.

"Admiral Nelson despised the Colonel," Sir Andrew continues, "apparently for causes related to the Colonel's military career. Also, Sylvester was an inveterate letter-writer to the Times, and the Admiral was upset at the anti-naval letters the Colonel wrote. He had exchanged sharp notes with Mr. Bassett-Hynde over the latter's history of some of the campaigns in India, and had suggested that Mr. Martin and his friends were the least desirable element of many despicable groups in the House of Commons.

"Finally, he and Lord Trent were bitter business rivals, and had engaged in a series of disagreements in letters to the Times over the years," says Sir Andrew, wondering if he has said too much. "If one of them wrote that the world was round, the other would insist that it is flat. In the lounge, they always took chairs beside the same end table, yet never spoke a word. Indeed, they were the pride of the club, in a manner of speaking."

"Oh?" you reply, startled.

"Indeed, yes, a great pride." Sir Andrew smiles for the first time since you began to question him. "What better proof of the integrity of our rules than to have two bitter enemies sit side by side for years, and never exchange a word nor take the slightest notice of each other?" *Turn to 499.*

367

"Good evening, sir," you say, rising to greet the gentleman. "I will try to waste as little of your time as possible."

"Thank you," he answers stiffly. He is a tall, lean, bespectacled man of impeccable taste and dress.

•*If you ask him what he saw, turn to 623.*
•*Otherwise, turn to 180.*

368

With a neat flurry of punches, you lay the valet out. With Watson, you begin to go through the papers, but they are so messy and confusing that you find nothing of interest. *Turn to 457.*

369

Battered and bruised, you awake to find Watson putting something back in his black bag. Once he is certain that you will be all right, he apologizes and hurries off to catch his train. *Reduce your Athletics bonus by one for the remainder of this adventure. Turn to 228.*

370

"The note was a death threat from Hamilton, the solicitor," you explain, "and is written in code. However, I didn't read the note until Mr. Hamilton had left the club, and your brother suggested that I wait and discuss the matter this morning."

"Mycroft is very cautious," Holmes mutters. "Well, with this evidence, I see two courses of action. You may get on with investigating other elements of the case, to present as thorough a package as possible, or you may push ahead and arrest the man. You have the address?"

You nod.

•*If you gather more evidence, turn to 405.*
•*If you confront Hamilton, turn to 555.*

371

· "Lord Hampton, the rival owner, arranged the drugging," you assert.

Holmes smiles. "And how did you decide that?" he asks. "You must have evidence to bring so serious a charge against a peer of the realm."

The relevant evidence includes Clues D, U, W, and X.

- *If you checked no clues or Clue D only, **turn to 150.***
- *If you checked Clue U but neither W nor X, **turn to 324.***
- *If you checked Clue X, but not U, **turn to 144.***
- *If you checked Clue W, but not U, **turn to 173.***
- *If you checked Clues U and W, but not X, **turn to 506.***
- *If you checked Clues U and X, **turn to 209.***

372

"I believe that the note was written by a foreign enemy of Colonel Sylvester," you explain. "The note is written in somewhat stilted language. It doesn't sound natural."

Holmes nods at this explanation. "Well," he answers, "if you are correct, we must pursue other evidence strongly, as there is no indication of who he might be, correct?" ***Turn to 405.***

373

"Yes," you say. "The Colonel practically drained the glass when he read the note." ***Turn to 104.***

374

"I told you I don't think it proper for me to wager," Raines snaps at you. "If you don't listen to my answers, there's no use my wasting the time to talk to you, is there? I'm a busy man." The trainer stomps away, obviously angry. You surmise that further attempts to talk to him would be useless. ***Turn to 570.***

375

"Yes, I have some, Mr. Holmes," you reply. "The bartender was very cooperative."

"Good," Holmes answers. "Carry on with the tests."

- *If you checked Decision 20, **turn to 534.***
- *Otherwise, **turn to 183.***

376

After making a note or two, you consider whether to ask Colonel Stuart any further questions.

- *If you ask him about his employees, **turn to 381.***
- *If you interview his employees, **turn to 481.***

Looking for a little physical exercise after the hours of talk, you walk to the room where Colonel Sylvester died. Sir Andrew points out his chair, but the body is gone. On the floor, you see a glass with a little brown liquid in the bottom. At your request, Dr. Watson hands you a small, clean jar from his bag, and you store the liquid safely away. *Turn to 134.*

378

Young Stanly is smiling as he sits down at your table and grabs a piece of bread. "Well, guv, I wish Mr. Holmes give me as easy jobs as you done today. Roscoe made one big tour around to the other blokes of his like, and they all give him money, and then he sat down at his table and paid out to all and sundry. I found me a place right beside it to hide and heard every word he said the whole time."

"Did he make a big payoff to anyone?" you ask.

"Nah, not no one. Whoever wagered Maiwand, wagered small. Only big money he give away didn't seem like it was no wager at all. Bloke named Oliver, groom to Colonel Stuart, come by and Roscoe gave him a lot of the ready. Couldn't tell how much cause Oliver just stuffed it in his pocket, but it was a nice touch. No word of any bet either. Well, thanks, guv," he adds when you slip him a pint. "Cheerio." *Check Clues I and C. Turn to 129.*

379

"So all that you require of a prospective member," you say, "are his willingness to abide by the club rules, and the ability to pay the club's charges?"

"Crudely put," Sir Andrew replies, "but I must admit that it is a fairly accurate interpretation."

"The rules for silence must be difficult for your staff to maintain," you suggest.

Sir Andrew nods, then adds: "But we pay much better than other clubs, and that can make up for a good deal of inconvenience."

•*If you ask about the staff members who dealt with Colonel Sylvester that day, turn to 240.*

•*Otherwise, turn to 119.*

380

You consider his answer a moment, hunting for the best phrasing of the next question.

•*If you ask why the horse ran badly, turn to 453.*

•*Otherwise, turn to 430.*

381

"Before I question your men, I should appreciate it if you'd tell me a little about them, Colonel," you say. "What are their duties, and what sort of men are they?" **Pick a number** and add your Communications bonus:

- *If 2-6, turn to 310.*
- *If 7-12, turn to 431.*

382

Before requesting your solution, Holmes listens to Colonel Stuart, who has some other information to offer. "Yes, Mr. Holmes, it's more clear than ever that Irish Star was drugged. Now that there has been time for it to wear off, the horse is back to his old energetic self."

- *If you checked Deduction 9, turn to 600.*
- *Otherwise, turn to 196.*

383

"Well, Mr. Holmes," you say, holding the clues in your mind. "I know that Dr. Watson is not easily distracted when he's writing — he ignored that telegram. In spite of that, he grabbed the newspaper and turned to the back page as soon as I handed it to him. Thus, his story must have reminded him of something that is always on the back page. Now what could that be?" **Pick a number** and add your Scholarship bonus:

- *If 2-8, turn to 216.*
- *If 9-12, turn to 566.*

384

"Is there one man you regularly place wagers with?" you ask Dr. Watson, as he pockets his winnings from the preceding race.

"I always bet with Roscoe," he answers.

Holmes seems to stiffen a bit at the name, then asks: "Doesn't the man's reputation concern you a little, Watson? There's been mention of Roscoe benefiting from some of the major upsets."

"Oh, there's that sort of talk about every such chap," Watson scoffs. "I know that Roscoe is honest with his customers. He always has the cash on hand to pay me, when I win, and one cannot say that of all of his rivals. And he has booths at every track, which I find convenient. Also, you often get better odds from a man who does a good deal of trade." **Pick a number** and add your Scholarship bonus:

- *If 2-7, turn to 363.*
- *If 8-12, turn to 548.*

385

"I have another sample, Mr. Holmes," you reply. "The Colonel's handkerchief was soaked in it, I believe, and I saved it."

"Let's test it, then," the detective suggests. *Pick a number and add your Scholarship bonus:*

- *If 2-5, turn to 391.*
- *If 6-12, turn to 577.*

386

"Did you blame the Colonel for your brother's death?" you ask.

"Blame the Colonel?" he repeats in astonishment. "Now, who am I to blame a colonel, sir? Besides, we know better in our family, we do, sir. We've always had two or three boys in every generation go for soldiers and sometimes they get killed. It hurts you, but that's what happens in a war, sir." *Turn to 269.*

387

You decide to let Hamilton go at this time. You tap your hands on the table and see Watson relax. "Thank you for your time, Mr. Hamilton," you say slowly, and the solicitor leaves.

As the door closes behind him, Watson leaps up in dismay. "How can you let him go like that?" he demands. "That note is practically a confession in itself."

"I'm not so certain," you answer. "He is a clever man — confronting him with the translated note might not force a confession, nor give us the information we need to prove that he caused Sylvester's death. I think I had better investigate more fully. Do you have other witnesses waiting, Sir Andrew?" you ask. *Turn to 334.*

388

Holmes has a wary look, but you accept your cousin's offer. As he hurries upstairs, you explain: "He has been so kind to me, Mr. Holmes, that I could hardly refuse when he offered help, could I?"

Holmes reluctantly agrees. Is the great detective a little jealous? Perhaps he resents being shut out of such an interesting case and would like to see all the loose ends joined as soon as possible.

Smiling, Watson returns with a big scrapbook. "I kept this for two or three years, after my return from Afghanistan," he explains. "Whenever the papers had an account of fighting in India or Afghanistan, I clipped it. Then, if I ran into any old comrades who knew more, I wrote out their comments and inserted them." With a flourish he opens it to one of the last items, and you read it eagerly.

Fighting in India

Units of the 17th Special brigade, under the command of Colonel Phillip Sylvester, were recently engaged with outlaw forces in the frontier region between India and Afghanistan. After several weeks of attempts to disperse the hostile forces, Colonel Sylvester found himself under attack on the evening of July 17, as his forces began to prepare their camp for the night.

Colonel Sylvester immediately responded to the threat, doubling his pickets and sending for assistance to the main forces in the area. Skirmishing continued all night, but the alert attitude of the British forces prevented a stronger attack. The enemy fled at dawn as the troops of the 17th and 19th brigades arrived to relieve Colonel Sylvester's command.

British casualties were very light, counting only one officer and one man killed, and five enlisted men wounded. The dead were among the messengers sent for help during the night attack on Sylvester's camp. The brutal and barbaric enemy captured those two devoted soldiers and tortured them to death in a manner shocking to even the most hardened veterans of the frontier army.

General Montgomery then ordered Colonel Sylvester to return to the Delhi district and to report the situation to the Governor-General. He also carried several captured chiefs into Delhi, in order that their crimes might be judged by the government. General Montgomery continued the pursuit of outlaw forces deep into the hills, and did not cease the operation until the enemy was scattered to the four winds.

British casulties included Lieutenant Terrence Saunders and Corporal John Smithson, killed in action, and Captain the Honourable Edward Trent, killed in an accident. Lieutenant Saunders is survived by his sister, Mary Victoria. Captain Trent is survived by his father, Major General Sir Gabriel Trent, his brothers Henry and Thomas, and his Uncle Lord Trent, the shipping magnate.

A second clipping, dated a few months later, mentions Colonel Sylvester's resignation. Beside the clippings, there is a note in Watson's almost indecipherable hand: "Sir H. says the deaths came from the Colonel's incompetence and cowardice, and that only mistaken kindness on the part of the high command permitted him to resign rather than face dismissal and disgrace by court-martial."

"Very good, Watson," Holmes says. "Now, if you will, get your gun, I would like you to accompany our friend today. When pursuing a murderer, there is always some danger." Watson readily agrees. *Check Deduction 18. Turn to 188.*

389
Pain blasts through your chest as Hamilton's bullet hits you. Before you realize more, you collapse, dead before you hit the ground. **The End**

390
"Most remarkable," mutters Watson. *Turn to 999.*

391

A second sample reveals that there was something unusual in the brandy, but you fail to isolate and identify it. *Turn to 104.*

392

"It sounds as if you did not like Colonel Sylvester," you say quietly. *Pick a number and add your Communication bonus:*

- *If 2-7, turn to 511.*
- *If 8-12, turn to 553.*

393

You have tested as thoroughly as you can.

"That's very significant isn't it, Holmes?" Watson asks. "The glass of brandy was poisoned but the bottle wasn't. That means the murderer had to be someone with easy access to Sylvester's glass."

The detective nods grimly.

- *If you checked Clue R, turn to 169.*
- *Otherwise, turn to 157.*

394

You decide that it would be silly. *Turn to 999.*

395

"How do you mean?" Wastson asks.

"Watson, our tests of the brandy in the glass revealed something odd, even if your cousin could not identify it," Holmes replies. "I discovered it when we did the tests, but I didn't say so at the time because I didn't want to prejudice his analysis."

You suppress your surprise that Holmes has withheld evidence from you.

"It is a West Indian plant extract, called Sunflight by those who know and use it," continues Holmes. "A powerful stimulant, a heavy dose almost certainly would cause a man like Sylvester to suffer a stroke. No, it was murder, and it will require more investigation to prove who did it." *Turn to 157.*

396

Hamilton proves too tough for you. As you try to fight him off, he topples an empty wine cask onto your head, and you collapse.

You return to consciousness to find an anxious Watson beside you, putting away the smelling salts. Your head and body ache, and worse, you know the murderer has escaped you. *Pick a number.*

- *If 2-6, turn to 630.*
- *If 7-12, turn to 631.*

397

At your request, Watson revives Roscoe so that you may question him. *Pick a number and add your Communications bonus:*

- *If 2-6, turn to 483.*
- *If 7-12, turn to 234.*

398

You read the label but have no idea what the drug is or what it would do to a horse who ingested it. *Turn to 126.*

399

"You never wager?" you ask, astonished. "I thought all racing people gave it a go now and again. How can you resist?" *Pick a number and add your Communication bonus:*

- *If 2-10, turn to 374.*
- *If 11-12, turn to 179.*

400

"There's only one more thing I'd like to see," you say. "Do you have any of the Colonel's St. Gabriel's brandy here?"

The valet nods and leads you to the bar. "He finished a bottle night before last, and I hadn't refilled the decanter when I heard he was dead."

All the bottles are sealed tightly, and close examination shows that the seals are identical; apparently none has been tampered with. You thank the valet for his help. *Turn to 457.*

401

You study Hamilton, wondering how far to push him.

- *If you ask his opionion of Colonel Sylvester, turn to 497.*
- *If you confront him, turn to 417.*
- *Otherwise, turn to 387.*

402

Lord Trent is an older man, thin, white-haired and dried out. His eyes are cold and hard. It will take tact to question him successfully.

- *If you ask him to describe what happened, turn to 428.*
- *Otherwise, turn to 303.*

403

Colonel Stuart is shown in by a steward; the bluff hearty face you remember appears pale and a little drawn by the day's events.

- *If you identified the person who drugged Irish Star, turn to 610.*
- *If you failed to identify the culprit, turn to 114.*

•*If Decision 6 is checked, turn to 105.*

The tackroom is sparkling clean, with the riding and grooming equipment set neatly in place. Bridles hang from hooks on the wall, saddles sit on supports, while blankets and other materials are folded neatly and set on shelves. Several large trunks hold smaller items. *Check Decision 6. Pick a number and add your Artifice bonus:*

•*If 2-7, turn to 513.*
•*If 8-12, turn to 640.*

405

"I think the first evidence you examine ought to be the Colonel's brandy," Holmes says. "We must prove that something was added to it, or any other evidence is useless."

Holmes has set up his apparatus. Together, you examine the brandy from the Colonel's glass, hoping to find and identify any foreign element in the brandy. *Pick a number and add your Scholarship bonus:*

•*If 2-7, turn to 164.*
•*If 8-12, turn to 577.*

406

Holmes eagerly welcomes you back to Baker Street. He barely allows you time to sit down and get something to drink before he demands: "Well, tell me now, who killed Colonel Sylvester?"

•*If you accuse Pierre Armand, turn to 118.*
•*If you accuse Lord Trent, turn to 469.*
•*If you accuse Henry Hamilton, turn to 502.*
•*If you accuse Sylvester's valet, turn to 112.*
•*If you accuse Tom Smithson, turn to 120.*
•*If you accuse Colonel Stuart, turn to 211.*

407

"Do you have any other information about the Frenchman?" you ask Holmes.

The detective pauses to think, then looks down a shelf and pulls down a directory of French businesses. From this tome, you learn that Pierre Armand was a major dealer in wine and spirits, one of the largest in France. He had large dealings in Britain, the Mediterranean and the West Indies, and travelled often to all these regions.

"A great traveller," Watson says, excited. "And the French are known as men who will seek revenge years after a wrong is done them. He could be our man." *Check Deduction 15. Turn to 305.*

408

After the horses warm up, the starter quickly gets them lined up at the white chalk and gives the signal for the start. The horses break, but Irish Star erupts more slowly than the others and doesn't respond when his rider whips him. The heavy favorite is running well behind the field, and the two or three leaders seem intent on building their advantage, apparently afraid that the grey's superiority will still emerge. Under the jockey's constant whipping, Irish Star tries to respond, but the big grey doesn't run well. Three horses cross the finish line in a bunch, and Watson's delighted yell reveals that Maiwand might have been the winner. Irish Star finishes ten lengths back, looking tired and almost bored by the effort.

"So much for science, Holmes," Watson laughs. "This will make my leg ache feel better on rainy days."

Holmes' eyes hold something of disdain as he looks back at the doctor. "Indeed, Watson?" he asks. "Has the bullet moved from your shoulder to your leg again? I should think it would be obvious even to your prejudiced view that something was very wrong with the running of that race."

You cut in before Watson can sputter out his obvious indignation. "Wrong, Mr. Holmes?" you ask, curious. *Pick a number and add your Communication bonus:*

● *If 2-5,* **turn to 286.**
● *If 6-12,* **turn to 663.**

409

Embarassed by your failure, you return to Baker Street and inform Holmes, who shakes his head in dismay.

"Well, well," he finally says, "at least we know who did it. I shall send a note to Lestrade. The authorities have some advantage over us in these matters, and they may be able to catch the villain before he leaves the country." Then, noticing how discouraged you look, Holmes continues. "Now, don't take on so. As Watson can tell you, guilty men have escaped my grasp as well. Knowing the guilty party is very useful, for it protects others from blame and may keep the villain from repeating his crime."

Somewhat comforted, you leave Baker Street, mulling over the mistakes that led to Hamilton's escape. You resolve that in your next case, you will know better, and bring the villain to justice yourself. And with any luck, another case will come your way soon. **The End**

410

"Do you have any notion who might have wished to interfere with Irish Star's performance?" you ask the Colonel.

"Why no, of course not!" he answers indignantly. "If I did, I would have confronted him and not come chasing after Mr. Holmes. Most likely some blackguard did it to make a profit on another horse."

2

Holmes interrupts your question with a sharp whistle, and a rather grubby looking youth in his early teens runs up and snaps to a dubious imitation of attention.

Holmes turns to you. "Young Stanly here is one of my irregulars," he explains. "He practically lives with the horses and knows everyone and everything that happens in and around the track. Assign him to watch one of your suspects, and you will be able to cover more ground." You accept the offer and give the lad his instructions.

•*If you have Roscoe followed,* **check Decision 1.**
•*If you have Fitzhugh and Bowser followed,* **check Decision 2.**
•*If you have Stuart's groom, John Oliver, followed,* **check Decision 3.**
Turn to 427.

411

You consider one other area of questions to ask Hamilton.

•*If you ask about the man who gave him the note,* **turn to 223.**
•*Otherwise,* **turn to 221.**

412

You thank Monsieur Armand for his time and help and leave the hotel. *Turn to 349.*

413

"You know, cousin," Watson says, "I still wonder about Lord Trent. Sitting where he did, he could have dropped something in Colonel Sylvester's drink without anyone knowing."

•*If you ask Holmes about Lord Trent,* **turn to 582.**
•*If not,* **turn to 177.**

You whisper to Dr. Watson: "Fall and act dazed when I stumble into you." You immediately trip and bang into the doctor. He crashes theatrically into a chair next to Roscoe's table and falls to the ground as if injured. *Pick a number and add your Artifice bonus:*

• *If 2-9, turn to 132.*
• *If 10-12, turn to 347.*

"As you wish," says Holmes. *Turn to 999.*

"What can you find about Hamilton?" you ask. "Is he too obscure, Mr. Holmes? The note makes him the prime suspect, certainly."

Holmes hands you the book and you read:

Henry Hamilton: Associate, Barnes, Grable and Anderson, 1881-1883. Queen's Council, Nassau, The Bahamas, 1883-1894. Independent practice, London, 1894—. Widower, m. Mary Victoria Saunders, 1880, d. 1894. Address, 417-B Hunter's Court, London.

Check Deduction 17. Turn to 356.

You nod sharply and notice Watson and Sir Andrew grow tense.

"But why did you write him this strange note, Mr. Hamilton?" you suddenly demand to know. "You tell him you wish his 'immediate death.' Odd sentiments for a respectable solicitor."

Hamilton stands, pacing the room like a beast in a cage, and stares at you in utter shock, his eyes almost popping out of his head. "You are clever, you fiend!" he shouts. "You broke the code, eh?'" A few moments of silence follow, as you and the others just stare at him, waiting for something to happen.

With great effort, he pulls himself together. "Well," he says, beginning to pace again. "Someone that clever deserves to hear the truth. When Colonel Sylvester was in the army, through cowardice and stupidity, he ordered two men on an unnecessary mission that ended in their being tortured to death. One of the men was the brother of my wife, and the blow so shocked her that it shattered her health and reason. The doctors said that a warmer climate might help her, so we sailed to the West Indies. There she got a little better, but she never grew whole and, finally, after twelve years of pain and sorrow, she passed away. I returned to England and found that I could raise only a small practice, and, at my station, I was unlikely to ever reach the heights of my profession."

You begin to feel compassion for Hamilton, however guilty he is.

"Still, this in itself would not have driven me to murder," he asserts, pausing to look you in the eye. "But I investigated Colonel Sylvester, and I found that he had grown rich, but he was still the same cruel, predatory man in his business career, grown rich from the very character defects that had destroyed my happiness. It was then that I resolved to kill him, and I succeeded. As he picked up the note from the floor, I put a powder in his brandy that would bring on the stroke that killed him. I am only sorry that it killed him outright, rather than condemning him to the years of agony that my poor wife suffered.

"You claim the right to be judge, jury and executioner?" Watson demands.

Hamilton stops pacing long enough to nod. ***Pick a number*** and *add your Perception bonus:*

- *If 2-10,* ***turn to 491.***
- *If 11-12,* ***turn to 569.***

418

Stanly smiles, preparing you for the climax of his story. "Yes, guv, Oliver led me a chase, he did, but I kept on him and he finally went to Roscoe's gambling table, and Roscoe gave him a big handful of money — without nothing being said about no wager. I snuck around behind where I heard everything they said, guv, and there weren't nothin' bout any wager." You thank Stanly for his good work and leave the pub. ***Check Clue I. Turn to 129.***

419

"Before we question the others, I wonder if you might be able to tell me a little bit more," you say to Sir Andrew. "You impress me as a man who pays close attention to what happens around you."

Sir Andrew hesitates for a moment, then nods in agreement. "Yes, that is reasonable, provided that everything you ask bears on the investigation."

- *If you ask about Colonel Sylvester,* ***turn to 344.***
- *Otherwise,* ***turn to 504.***

420

You ask another question or two about Hamilton's background, trying to find some way to explore the man's emotional state.

- *If you ask what he saw in the lounge,* ***turn to 496.***
- *Otherwise,* ***turn to 245.***

421

You decide that some subtle message is hidden in the note and resolve to figure it out. *You may reread the note at 276.* **Check Decision 22.**

●*If you cannot "break" the code,* **turn to 438.**
●*If you successfully "break" the code,* **turn to 519.**

422

You find a small medicine bottle wrapped in a man's handkerchief hidden between the shutter and the outside wall. Turning it around, you look at the label. **Turn to 628.**

423

While you think that Colonel Stuart threatened Sylvester, you wonder whether it would do any good to show him the note and ask him about it.

●*If you show Colonel Stuart the note and ask an explanation,* **turn to 229.**
●*Otherwise,* **turn to 326.**

424

"I cannot see what would tell me that," you admit to Holmes. "Would you explain?"

"Yes, Holmes," Watson adds, "How did I tip you off?"

"It is simple," Holmes replies. "When you write, Watson, you are very diligent—not much distracts you from your work. Yet when the newspaper came, you grabbed it and looked at the back page at once. So whatever you would find on the back page must be related strongly to the story you are writing, as it concerned you more than the telegram." **Turn to 213.**

425

You wonder if Armand could have learned about Sunflight during his residence in the West Indies.

●*If you ask Armand about Sunflight,* **turn to 532.**
●*Otherwise,* **turn to 187.**

426

"No, thank you, cousin," you say politely. "But I would be very pleased if you would accompany me today. I will need a stout heart beside me, before the day's work is done."

Watson's short-lived look of disappointment disappears, and he eagerly joins you and Holmes in planning the day. **Turn to 188.**

"Well, you seem settled into the case," Holmes adds, looking at his watch. "Be careful in this matter. Do not make any charges or draw undue attention to what happened until you obtain solid evidence. Hints of a charge in a case like this are every bit as bad for the reputations involved as a conviction itself. Unless you can force the guilty to confess, I suggest that you merely assemble the evidence and present me with your conclusions when I return to London. I will send you a note when I get back to Baker Street. Watson, meet me on the train platform, if you please. Good luck." The detective turns away, then swings back, as one last thought strikes him. "Remember the dog who didn't bark in the night," he says.

"What do you mean, Holmes?" Watson demands, before you can phrase your own question.

"It occurred to me, Watson," Holmes explains, "that whoever arranged for Irish Star to lose may not have intended Maiwand to win." He turns and walks off with his characteristic long stride.

•*If you join Dr. Watson as he collects his winnings,* **turn to 489.**
•*If you go straight to the stable with Colonel Stuart,* **turn to 565 and Check Decision 4.**

428

"Thank you for your time," you begin. "Could you tell me anything of what Colonel Sylvester did in the lounge this afternoon?" *Pick a number and add your Communication bonus:*
•*If 2-8,* **turn to 463.**
•*If 9-12,* **turn to 626.**

429

You wonder what Holmes thought of the late Colonel Sylvester. If he were willing to tell you, his opinion would be of great value. There are few better judges of human nature than Mr. Sherlock Holmes.

•*If you ask Holmes his opinion of Sylvester,* **turn to 444.**
•*Otherwise,* **turn to 611.**

430

"Thank you for your time," you tell Raines. "I appreciate your candor, knowing what a busy man you are."

"My pleasure," the trainer answers. ***Turn to 570.***

431

"There is little to say about them, so far as I know," Colonel Stuart says. "Henry Raines, my trainer, is one of the best in the country and works for many owners of the highest station. He would lose far too much were he ever foolish enough to intentionally lose a race. What nonsense! My groom, John Oliver, has been with me for two years and has always been loyal, even when I've been tardy with his pay."

•*If you ask about the groom, **pick a number** and add your Communication bonus:*

  •*If 2-6, **turn to 572.***
  •*If 7-12, **turn to 268.***
•*Otherwise, **turn to 481.***

432

While much of the crowd left after the feature race, many people remain, chatting about the way the races were run. A sign identifies Roscoe's table, which is the busiest by far. ***Pick a number*** *and add your Observation bonus:*

•*If 2-7, **turn to 592.***
•*If 8-12, **turn to 166.***

433

You hesitate to ask the first question, marveling at the enormity of your questioning Sherlock Holmes in a murder investigation.

•*If you ask Holmes what he saw when Sylvester died, **turn to 619.***
•*Otherwise, **turn to 429.***

434

"I see," you mutter. "And was the Colonel successful as a businessman?'

"Quite successful," Sir Andrew says hurriedly. "Though I must admit that some have suggested that his methods left a little to be desired. Nothing you could point to for certain, you understand, or we would not have granted him membership in the club, but just a willingness to take every advantage."

"But nothing to stop his membership," you repeat.

•*If you ask about the club's rules, **turn to 101.***
•*Otherwise, **turn to 379.***

435

"Now you've studied his desk," Holmes says. "Is he writing letters or a story?"

- *If you say, "Letters," turn to 338.*
- *If you say, "A story," turn to 512.*

436

"No," you say after reflection. "I doubt that we shall learn anything useful there." *Turn to 614.*

437

You approach Irish Star's jockey and introduce yourself.

"Colonel Stuart hired me to look into the race for him," you explain. "Would you care to talk about it?" *Pick a number and add your Communication bonus:*

- *If 2-7, turn to 456.*
- *If 8-12, turn to 503.*

438

The coded message has baffled you. You hope that it does not have any relevance to Colonel Sylvester's death.

- *If you are at the Diogenes Club, turn to 648.*
- *If you are at Baker Street, turn to 315.*

439

As you finish your supper in the pub, young Stanly peeks in, looking for you. It takes a word from you before the proprietor allows him entry. Stanly hurries to your table.

- *If you checked Decision 1, turn to 378.*
- *If you checked Decision 2, turn to 307.*
- *If you checked Decision 3, turn to 160.*

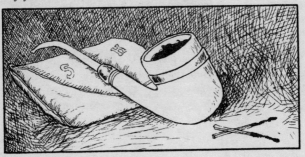

Eagerly you consider what the decoded message means, and how best to use it.

•*If you checked Decision 20,* ***turn to 327.***
•*Oherwise,* ***turn to 319.***

441

You cannot identify the liquid which soaked the handkerchief. Preoccupied with the death scene, you lay the useless piece of cloth aside. ***Turn to 207.***

442

"Oh, Watson," Holmes continues, a mischievous smile on his lips, "in your story, did you tell of the dog who did not bark in the night?"

"Indeed, Holmes, it is one of my key points," Dr. Watson notes.

"As well it should be." Holmes turns towards you. "It was an important teaching point, too. When you investigate something, look for what isn't there or didn't happen as well as what was or did. Watson, now that we have fully distracted you from your writing, shouldn't you read the telegram?"

"Telegram?" Watson says in a distracted voice. "Oh, yes, the telegram." He rips open the envelope and reads it quickly. "Why, Holmes, it is from Sir Henry Baskerville. He invites us for the weekend, noting that he has something to show you well worth your time."

"He does, does he?" Holmes answers. "I doubt that, or he would have come up to London in person. More probably he feels he still owes us hospitality for that little matter we solved some time ago. Well, as you received the telegram, Watson, you must send our refusal."

"Indeed I will not, Holmes," replies your cousin. "Sir Henry provided us with a most interesting investigation, you must admit. Surely we can spare him a weekend. The fresh air will do you good, and you have no case to tie you to London at this time."

"Oh, very well, Watson," Holmes sighs. "I can see I will have no peace until I agree. We can take a late train Friday afternoon." Then the detective busies himself with his pipe once more.

"I have only one regret, Holmes," Watson adds, after giving the page the reply to take to the telegraph office.

"What is that, Watson?"

"You will miss your chance to instruct me in the art of picking winning race horses — on Friday we had planned to go to the track."

Holmes pulls his Bradshaw down from the bookcase and looks up the train schedule, then nods. "Not at all, Watson," he says. "We can catch the train at a station near the racing grounds. Unless something holds up the card, we should be able to see the feature and have time to collect our winnings afterwards."

"You are going to the races, Mr. Holmes?" you ask in some surprise. "I didn't know you indulged in that pleasure."

"I seldom do," Holmes answers, "but Watson needs a lesson or two from a logical mind to cut his losses. The race on Friday will provide an excellent demonstration. I am certain which horse will win, while Watson has his own ideas in the matter."

"Why don't you join us?" Watson suggests. "Then I shall have a witness when I show Holmes that pure logic is not the solution to every problem. Meet us here at noon — that is all right with you, isn't it Holmes?"

"Certainly," the detective agrees, but from his expression you see his mind is drifting away toward some other problem. As quickly as politeness permits, you bid them good day and leave.

Some small matters delay you on Friday, and Holmes and Watson are boarding their cab as you run up Baker Street to meet them. The driver is busy piling their luggage on top of the groaner.

"You almost missed us," Watson laughs, waving to you. "It should be an interesting afternoon. Holmes is certain he already knows the winner in the feature and mocks my choice. Get in, and let's be off."

You do not need a second invitation, and soon the three of you are rattling through the streets, where most of the populace is concerned with far more serious business than a day at the races. You pay little attention to the London crowds, though, given a rare chance to talk with the world's greatest consulting detective.

"How is your education progressing?" Holmes asks courteously, although you have a feeling that he can read your limited success from your looks and attitude.

After a moment, you frame a reply. "I am doing well enough, I suppose. I have had some success in finding missing things and uncovering evidence, but I have as much trouble as the police in matters where there are a number of likely suspects. I suppose it will take years for me to acquire your knack of cutting to the heart of the matter, Mr. Holmes."

"It is a lifetime's study," Holmes agrees, "and even then, there will be more than one time when you prove yourself a fool. That has happened to me, as Watson has told the world in his tales. But one thing to consider — wherever you are and whatever you happen to be doing, keep your eyes open for things that might lead to crime. My greatest successes have come in matters where I have had an idea in advance that something was going to happen, and have been able to take steps to prevent the crime or catch the perpetrator in the act. That was how Watson and I saved Dr. Roylott's stepdaughter from his evil designs and solved other cases."

"Surely you downgrade your genius, Holmes," Watson interjects. "You make the most difficult tasks seem simple, you know."

"Not at all," Holmes insists. "But if you know a wealthy man has an heir desperate for money, you can prevent a crime by a word in the heir's ear. Or if we should see a notorious gambler bet heavily on a long shot today, we would protect the purity of the turf with a word to the stewards. A man who would make a career of detection must always have his eyes open to everything around him. It is the only way to do one's job."

"Oh, enough talk of detection, Holmes!" Watson interrupts. "Why don't you tell my cousin about the race this afternoon? Explain to him why your logical and scientific approach to handicapping will do better than my foolish 'hunch.'" Watson laughs merrily, even as Holmes frowns.

"Watson," Holmes snaps, "you should know better than to mock logic. You must admit that your attempts at picking winning horses have cost you half your pension."

"Now, now, Holmes," Watson mutters, "I've done better than that."

"What horse do you favor this afternoon, Mr. Holmes?" you ask.

"I am going to bet on Irish Star," the detective answers. "He is a very strong horse and runs consistently well. He doesn't belong on the same track with the rest of the field — it is only an odd quirk in the conditions that allow him to run. From every point of past performance and current condition, there is simply no way that the horse can fail to win."

"I see," you say, impressed. "Then why won't my cousin back Irish Star as well?"

"Dr. Watson," Holmes says loftily, "intends to bet on a horse called Maiwand, because it is named for the battle where he was wounded. He considers it a lucky omen, I believe." Watson squirms slightly, although his usual bulldog expression suggests that he will not change his mind.

•*If you ask Watson about Irish Star,* **turn to 170.**
•*Otherwise,* **turn to 603.**

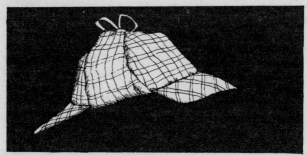

443

"A fine summation of the evidence," Holmes says quietly, "but get to the crux of the matter. Whom do you accuse of drugging Irish Star?"

•*If you accuse the jockey,* **turn to 360.**
•*If you accuse Henry Raines, the trainer,* **turn to 514.**
•*If you accuse Bowser & Fitzhugh,* **turn to 591.**
•*If you accuse John Oliver,* **turn to 140.**

444

Holmes shakes his head. "I did not know Sylvester well, and did not wish to know him better. Still, I have some notes on him in my Commonplace Books at Baker Street, for I thought he might prove to be either a client or a target one day. A mean, shifty man, despite his fine appearance." *Turn to 611.*

445

You look closely at the glass and note that there is a little brandy in the bottom. At your request, Watson hands you a clean jar carried in his medical bag, and you empty the contents of the brandy glass into it. *Pick a number and add your Observation bonus:*

- *If 2-6,* **turn to 207.**
- *If 7-12,* **turn to 343.**

446

Holmes listens patiently to your of accusations regarding Hamilton's guilt, then shakes his head. "You have the right man, but you need more evidence to make a case. You have shown that he could have known of the drug, but you present no motive. However, perhaps that can be remedied."

- *If you want Holmes' help,* **turn to 546.**
- *If you want to try again to solve the mystery on your own,* **turn to 237.**

447

"I have decided the note was probably irrelevant," you tell Holmes."How can a note that Colonel Sylvester failed to read bear on the question of who killed him?"

Holmes looks surprised, then nods. "Well," he says, "if that is your conclusion, we had better get to work analyzing other evidence." *Turn to 405.*

448

"Colonel Stuart hired me to investigate for him," you explain. *Turn to 999.*

"Admiral," you begin, "did you notice anything of what Colonel Sylvester did before he died? Anything out of the ordinary?"

"Why, no, I cannot say it was anything out of the ordinary," he answers, "and if I admit looking at it, I may get thrown out of the club for prying." He tosses a sidelong glance at Sir Andrew, but adds: "I shall tell you if you like."

●*If you ask him to go on,* **turn to 231.**
●*Otherwise,* **turn to 605.**

"If you want to learn more about Hamilton, you might visit his old offices," Watson suggests. "Though after so many years, it's probably a waste of time. I doubt that any of his associates would remain."

●*If you visit Hamilton's old offices,* **turn to 564.**
●*Otherwise,* **turn to 158.**

"My God, what a tragic story!" you gasp. "I certainly pity the poor man. The brother must have suffered a horrifying death for it to affect his sister so."

"Very horrible," Grable agrees. "He was an officer with our forces in India. Due to the blunders of his commander, he was captured and killed by the barbarians, who tortured him to death in the most frightening way imaginable. Some fool told the girl how her brother died. The man whose blunder caused the lad's death, Colonel Sylvester, died suddenly yesterday, I read." ***Check Deduction 23. Turn to 158.***

"Thank you for speaking to me," you begin. If anything, Mycroft fills you with even more awe than does his more famous brother. You have heard that his ungainly appearance hides his shrewdness and powerful intellect.

●*If you ask what he saw when the Colonel died,* **turn to 260.**
●*Otherwise,* **turn to 130.**

"Do you have any idea why Irish Star ran so badly today?" you ask the trainer.

Raines hesitates for a moment, then shakes his head. "I really don't, unless Colonel Stuart is right, and someone drugged the horse.

I was certain, as sure as I ever have been, that my horse was going to win. I swear."

- *If you ask why he was certain of victory,* **turn to 202.**
- *Otherwise,* **turn to 430.**

454

Once more Sir Andrew looks at his list, pausing to think. "If you judge it worth the time, I think we had better send for Sir Alexander Bassett-Hynde next," he says. "He mentioned that he had an engagement this evening and is most displeased at having to wait."

- *If you talk to Sir Alexander,* **turn to 367.**
- *Otherwise,* **turn to 461.**

455

- *If Decision 7 is checked,* **turn to 105.**
  You begin to search Irish Star's stall. It is a snug place, solidly built. The straw is fresh and clean, and the feedbox and water buckets are clean and ready for the horse. **Check Decision 7. Pick a number** *and add your Artifice bonus:*

- *If 2-7,* **turn to 513.**
- *If 8-12,* **turn to 640.**

456

"Talk about it?" he asks, scoffing. "What's to talk about? The horse didn't have any run in him and got his tail whipped. It happens, even with the best. Excuse me; my friends need a drink." He pointedly turns his back on you. **Turn to 439.**

457

Certain that you and Watson will accomplish nothing more there, you leave Sylvester's flat and take a hansom back to Baker Street. **Turn to 406.**

458

With Watson, you come to the building in Mayfair where Colonel Sylvester maintained a flat. It is a well-built building, and even the fittings of the entry and stairs show that the home belongs to men of great wealth. A porter shows you how to get up to Sylvester's rooms, but there is no answer when you and Watson knock. **Pick a number** *and add your Observation bonus:*

- *If 2-5,* **turn to 457.**
- *If 6-12,* **turn to 218.**

459

"What a horrible tale," you mutter. "How did the poor man die?"
you inquire, leaning forward eagerly.

Grable looks at you sharply. "And what would that have to do with
hiring poor Hamilton as a solicitor? I have no time to waste on such
matters, sir. Jones, show these gentlemen out."

The clerk shows you to the door with little ceremony, and you and
Watson must decide on your next step. *Turn to 158.*

460

"Of course," Holmes adds, "while knowing who drugged the
horse is important, it is critical to prove who paid him to do the deed.
Oliver will likely have little chance to repeat his crime, but his master
might strike again through some other agent."

Once more you run through the evidence and try to summarize the
conclusions that will lead to your accusation. As you run on, Holmes
interrupts. "But tell us," he urges. "Who bribed John Oliver to drug
Irish Star?"

•*If you accuse Colonel Stuart, turn to 598.*
•*If you aaccuse Lord Hampton, turn to 371.*
•*If you accuse Bowser and Fitzhugh, turn to 325.*
•*If you accuse Roscoe, turn to 254.*

461

"Who is next?" you ask Sir Andrew.

"Lord Trent, the man who customarily sat next to the Colonel. Do
you wish to talk to him?"

•*If you ask to see Lord Trent, turn to 402.*
•*Otherwise, turn to 168.*

462

"From all accounts, your cousin was a man to avoid," you say, and
Stuart nods.

•*If you asked him why he came to the club, turn to 151.*
•*Otherwise, turn to 171.*

463

"Why, what a question!" Lord Trent replies, apparently upset. "I
have better things to do than to violate club rules by spying upon my
fellow members."

After that outburst, he composes himself and continues. "There
did seem to be a lot of bustle and activity around his chair, before he
collapsed. Waiters and others came to his chair, but I did not pay

much attention. When he collapsed, I looked up; I was very disturbed at him for breaking the rule of silence. I saw him fall on the floor. Sensing that this was one occasion that I should pay a little attention, I knelt and felt for a pulse, but he was already gone." *Turn to 303*.

464

Fumbling with Watson's penknife, you fail to pick the lock and cannot open the door. *Turn to 457*.

465

You agree to Sir Andrew's suggestion and follow him to the bar, the note half-forgotten in your hand. Sir Andrew tells the bartender to answer anything you ask.

You ask how the service is organized. "I am especially curious," you add, "how you can promptly deliver the proper drinks to members when there is a ban on speaking in the club."

"Aye, sir, that took some organizing, it did," he answers. "We had considerable troubles the first year or two the club was open. Now it's easy enough. When a man comes in, he leaves a note of what he's drinking that day at the door. Then, when he wants something, he pushes a buzzer under the arm of his chair, and a waiter takes it straight to him. We do so very quickly too, sir, for these gents are hardly the most patient types."

"You keep a wide variety of drinks, I suppose?" you ask.

"Well, we do and we don't," he answers ambiguously. "I only buy a few things. Most of the members bring their own favorites, and I keep them ready. The men who would belong to a club like this one usually are a little different in what they drink, also, you understand, sir." You nod.

•*If you ask what Colonel Sylvester drank, turn to 482*.
•*Otherwise, turn to 122*.

466

"Hold on a moment, Colonel, please," you interrupt. "Before we give this beauty to the law, I should like more answers from him. Who paid you to drug Irish Star?" you demand of Oliver.

"I won't tell nobody that! Never!" the groom answers with surprising spunk. "I don't take no man down with me, no sir, and it'd be worth my life to do so." He quails when you and Colonel Stuart step towards him, but then adds: "If you goes a bit easy on me, I will get you what's left of the drug." As the Colonel nods, he fetches a small medicine bottle from its hiding place under a blanket and gives it to you. *Turn to 628*.

As you and Watson hurry down the alley, you see Hamilton turn into a cross alley leading back to the main road. You give chase, but when you turn into the alley, he has disappeared. You follow it to the main road, but the murderer is nowhere in sight.

"Where is he?" Watson asks, then adds: "He must have hidden in one of the shops," pointing to the three buildings lying between the alley and street.

The other side of the alley is blocked by an abandoned warehouse; the doors are boarded up and obviously impassable. You stop to think. The first building has a back door opening onto the alley at ground level, the second has a pair of wide flat doors leading down into its cellar, while the third has doors at both ground and basement levels.

- *If you search the first building, **turn to 558.***
- *If you enter the second, **turn to 561.***
- *If you enter the third, **turn to 194.***
- *If you stand at the corner and watch the front of the shops, **turn to 108.***

Just as you and Watson are about to give up looking for Hamilton, a hansom rattles past in the street, and an urchin cries: "That's Martin's cab — he's the one your man left in!"

You hurry to the cab. "Where did you leave your last passenger?" you demand.

"What's it to you?" the driver replies, almost snarling. "'e paid 'is fare."

"The man's a murderer," you reply. "If you don't want a sentence for helping him to escape..."

That threat gets the cabbie's attention. "'ere, 'ere, mate," he says, calming you. "I didn't know the bloke was no murderer, swear I 'ad no idea. You woudn't shop a poor workin' man just because he accidentally took the trade of a criminal, not you, mate."

"Well, take us where you took him, then," Watson demands. "And snap to it!"

"Won't do you no good if I did," he replies. "I took 'im to the station, and 'e 'opped the local train. But maybe we can cut 'im off. That train is just on the city line. If 'e wants to leave London, 'e'll 'ave to change at the Riverside station, three miles from 'ere. And if the train is just a mite late there, why, you'll 'ave 'im in a box, so you will."

"Then go!" Watson urges. *Turn to 578.*

469

"Lord Trent murdered Colonel Sylvester," you assert. "He hated him for years, and he certainly had every opportunity to put something in the brandy."

Holmes shakes his head. "Trent lacks the West Indian background to connect him to the drug, and I doubt the depth of his motive. The men were not business rivals. In fact, Lord Trent is probably distressed at Sylvester's demise — he enjoyed their correspondance in the Times." *Turn to 296.*

470

Holmes nods as you explain that you suspect Oliver because he warned his brother against betting on Irish Star when everyone expected the horse to win. "That is a reasonable conclusion," he admits, "although I should like to see more solid evidence. Connecting Oliver to the drug or to a payoff would be more more profitable."

•*If you want to try to solve the mystery again without being given the solution,* **turn to the Prologue** *and begin anew.*

•*Otherwise,* **turn to 460.**

"Did you get along well with your cousin?" you ask.

Stuart looks a little surprised, then nods. "Well, that's a fair question, as he died so suddenly. We did not get along well, I'm afraid, though I was his only close relation. He was a hard-natured man who neither liked nor trusted anyone; he probably felt that they were all talking about him behind his back. And there was little to like or respect about him — he was a coward and a fool when he was in India, and a cheating, dishonest businessman since he returned to England. Yet when I made some effort to be kind, he distrusted me, and then insulted me by reading his will to me."

"What about his will?" you ask, hiding your eagerness.

"Why, he almost accused me of wanting to murder him. In the will, it specifies that I will not inherit a penny if he dies in any suspicious manner, not until someone else is found responsible. If I weren't in such desperate financial straits, I'd have told him to leave his fortune to his cat!" *Turn to 659.*

472

You have never heard of St. Gabriel's Brandy. *Pick a number and add your Intuition bonus:*

- If 2-7, *turn to 609.*
- If 8-12, *turn to 634.*

473

You manage to open the lock, and you and Watson quietly enter Colonel Sylvester's flat. No one is in the hall or sitting room, but you follow the noise to an office at the rear. There you find a solidly built man, dressed as a valet, dumping papers out of files, frantically scanning them and then throwing them into the fire.

- If you attack him, *turn to 549.*
- If you speak to him, *turn to 292.*

474

"Did you know Colonel Sylvester, or know anything of him?" you ask Hamilton.

"Oh no, I never had any contact with him or heard of him," Hamilton answers. "My employer may well have chosen me for that reason, to avoid the awkwardness of recognition."

- *If you have Clue Y, turn to 206.*
- *Otherwise, pick a number and add your Intuition bonus:*
  - *If 2-7, turn to 411.*
  - *If 8-12, turn to 226.*

475

The messenger returns, bringing Mycroft Holmes with him. Mycroft is a tall, stout man with penetrating grey eyes (like his brother), an imperious air and an expression of introspection, as if figuring a mathematical puzzle in his head all the time.

"Good evening, Mycroft," Sir Andrew says. "I appreciate your coming. This young gentleman is looking into the death of poor Sylvester; it seems your brother is occupied with other matters this evening. Both Sherlock and I thought that you might have noticed something of interest."

"Very well," Mycroft uncomfortably agrees, settling himself into the only chair big enough for him. *Turn to 452.*

476

Colonel Stuart quickly reads the note, and when he finishes, you ask: "Did you mean this as a threat when you sent it to Colonel Sylvester?"

Colonel Stuart's complexion turns a rich purple, and he begins to raise his stick towards you. "What kind of an idiotic question is that?" he demands, storming from the room after Dr. Watson rises to counter his threat.

"A little tact is sometimes useful," Sir Andrew suggests tartly. "I hope Stuart did not know anything useful, for we shall never learn of it now." *Turn to 454.*

477

"No, Mr. Holmes," you answer. "There was something in the glass. There must have been! It's only logical. Perhaps it was a chemical not powerful enough to kill him with just a small sip." *Turn to 395.*

478

"Who told you that Irish Star wouldn't run well?" you ask the doctor.

"Oh, Tom Oliver, a waiter at my club. When he saw me looking over the entries this morning, he warned me about the horse."

"A waiter at your club, Watson?" Holmes asks, feigning disbelief. "But if he is so expert on form, surely he wouldn't have to spend his days at such menial labor?"

Watson shudders as Holmes chuckles, then snaps: "The man has connections at the track, nonetheless. Holmes, you must admit you have found sources in more unlikely places many a time." This riposte leads Holmes to a discussion of some of the more unlikely witnesses he has encountered over the years. **Check Clue T. Turn to 603.**

479

"Have you read the note you found on the body?" Holmes asks.

"No, sir," you answer, "I'm not convinced that it has any relevance. After all, the Colonel failed to read it."

"I think you should read it," Watson urges. "It might tell us something useful about the man."

•*If you read the note,* **turn to 361.**
•*Otherwise,* **turn to 295.**

480

Having gathered all the evidence you seem likely to get, you return home to await the arrival of Mr. Holmes and Dr Watson. You turn your mind to useful reading of the sort Holmes recommends, hoping to avoid constantly rehashing the case, but night after night you still find this case a distraction. Have I uncovered the pertinent information and interpreted it logically, you wonder.

It is a relief to receive a note from Mr. Holmes, informing you of his return and asking you to come around to Baker Street and give him your solution. You waste no time going to see him. Watson and Colonel Stuart are with the detective when you arrive, the latter willing to explain some of the unusual elements of the case.

•*If you simply want to name the culprit,* **turn to 312.**
•*If you want to review the evidence first and present a more detailed portrait of the crime to Holmes,* **turn to 382.**

481

Colonel Stuart leads you to othere stables. Here, he rents two stalls, both of which are clean and well-tended. A neat tack room holds a cot, where the groom sleeps.

Stuart's two men are waiting for your arrival. Henry Raines, the trainer, is a thin, dried out man with a sharp nose and narrow eyes. He has the air of a man who knows his business. Beside him stands John Oliver, the groom, dressed in work clothes. He has a open, red face and seems a very ordinary sort of working man.

"This gentleman is a detective," Colonel Stuart explains. "It is obvious that something was done to slow Irish Star today, and I have hired him to investigate the matter."

"Investigate?" Raines snaps. "Does that mean you think we did ought to the horse, sir?" His eyes flash.

"No, no," Stuart assures him. "I shall explain. You had better start with Oliver," the Colonel says to you, and at a nod, John Oliver follows you into an empty stall.

"Now, you must help me Mr. Oliver, for I am terribly ignorant about the care of racehorses and the duties of the various men around them," you begin, anxious to put him at ease. "I must have solid information to stand a chance of unraveling this case."

"Sure thing, Guv," the groom eagerly replies. "I'm always glad to help the gentry. Just shoot your questions and I'll tell you anything you need to know."

"Thank you," you answer. "I shall be certain to tell Colonel Stuart how helpful you are. First, exactly what are your duties as groom?"

"I do what you might expect, guv," says Oliver. "I muck out the stall and lay down fresh straw in the morning. I feed the horse and I cools him out sometimes. Now on race days like today, Mr. Raines has a boy of his who walks him after the race, so I can have everything shipshape when he come back to his stall. And o' course I groom him couple times a day, keep the big boy pretty as a picture, I do."

●*If you have Clue T,* **turn to 644.**
●*Otherwise,* **turn to 495.**

482

"I understand the late Colonel Sylvester drank brandy," you say. "Did he drink from your stock?"

"Oh no, sir, not him," the steward laughs before growing embarassed. "He only drank St. Gabriel's, which is made in a French monastery." *Pick a number* **and add your Scholarship bonus:**

●*If 2-9,* **turn to 472.**
●*If 10-12,* **turn to 117.**

483

"Why behave so violently when someone asks to look at your client list?" you ask. "Have you something to hide?"

"Hide? Not me, Guv'nor, not me," Roscoe insists. "I just don't like no one looking at me papers. I've had troubles over the like before, when wives set a man to snoop after their hubbies. Give a man a break."

You get nothing more from Roscoe. His clerk helps him stand as Dr. Watson hurries to catch his train. *Turn to 228.*

484

"I suppose very few people bought such a rare vintage," you mutter, and Amber agrees, without offering details.

●*If you ask to see a list of clients,* **turn to 107.**
●*Otherwise,* **turn to 528.**

485

"I am considering a visit to Amber's, the dealer who sells the Colonel's brandy," you say.

"Oh. Do you think someone substituted a poisoned bottle for the Colonel's at the club?"

●*If you go to Amber's,* **turn to 182.**
●*Otherwise,* **turn to 436.**

486

"I just laid the money, you see, like any man in my trade would," the fellow snaps. Pushing Roscoe further might lead to trouble, you sense. *Turn to 293.*

487

"Has anyone offered to buy Irish Star?" you ask.

"Indeed, yes!" Stuart snaps, "and fool that I am, I rejected the offer. Lord Hampton offered to buy the horse Tuesday last, just after Irish Star ran against his champion, Queensland. He offered about half what I would say the horse is worth, but warned me he would slash the offer if Irish Star did not win today, for he wanted the field clear for Maiwand. Now I am afraid I shall have to sell the beauty at a much-reduced price." You nod in sympathy. *Check Clue U. Turn to 376.*

488

You begin to ask Holmes about Hamilton, but before you can get the words out he hands you a directory of London solicitors. You read the entry:

Henry Hamilton: Associate, Barnes, Grable and Anderson, 1881-1883. Queen's Council, Nassau, The Bahamas, 1883-1894. Independent practice, London, 1894—. Widower, m. Mary Victoria Saunders, 1880, d. 1894. Address, 417-B Hunter's Court, London.

Check Deduction 17. Turn to 356.

489

After telling Colonel Stuart that you will join him at his stable in a few minutes, you accompany Dr. Watson as he walks to the tables to collect his winnings. One or two men are seated at each table, with big ledgers in front of them. They make various marks in their books as they accept winning tickets from their successful customers, few in number as far as you can see. One table, protected by an awning, sports a large sign that reads:

ROSCOE'S, THE OLD ESTABLISHMENT

Watson hurries towards Roscoe's booth, stopping to speak to a man who hurries from table to table, collecting from each. Watson taps him on the shoulder.

"You should be paying out, Roscoe, not collecting," Dr. Watson says teasingly, adding: "Roscoe, this is my cousin."

"Glad to meet the doctor's family, for he's one of my best customers," the man says, adding a booming laugh. Roscoe is powerfully built, though running to fat, and wears a rough brown coat and derby hat. "Well, doctor," he adds, "I'm always glad to see you, though I'm just as happy that your friend Holmes isn't with you. That bloke makes me fair nervous — he seems to know every wicked thought that comes in me head before I think it meself." Roscoe laughs again. *Check Clue C.*

•*If you ask Roscoe about his winnings, turn to 507.*
•*Otherwise, turn to 293.*

490

Holmes face turns to stone as you stumble through your explanation of Hamilton's involvement and guilt — the detective is obviously very disappointed in you.

"How can you make that charge?" he demands. "You have no real evidence to back it up." *Turn to 296.*

491

Suddenly, in the course of his feverish pacing, Hamilton leaps through one of the windows! *Turn to 328.*

"Cousin John," you say slowly to Watson. "Would you look at him and see how you think he died?" The doctor nods grimly, then kneels and quickly examines the corpse. Then he rises and wipes his hands on a handkerchief before speaking.

"You know," he finally says, "I would think on examining him that the poor man suffered a fatal stroke. He is the sort of man prone to strokes, you understand, and he displays all the visible signs." *Turn to 445.*

"I heard that you offered to buy Irish Star very recently," you say slowly, watching for a reaction.

Lord Hampton raises one eyebrow in surprise, then laughs softly. "I always say that there are no secrets around a racetrack," he says in a low voice. "I knew that Colonel Stuart was in financial trouble and offered to buy the horse. I thought I might get a bargain, and now I shall likely strike an even better deal. I've heard that if he didn't win the purse, the stewards might take legal action to force the Colonel pay his track debts. But I gave him fair warning. I told him I would pay 500 pounds before the race or 250 after. A wager between us, you might say." **Check** *Clue U. Turn to 317.*

You explain to Holmes that you think the note a threat from Colonel Stuart. The detective shakes his head. "Oh come now," he says, "is that likely? Even if the Colonel were to send such a note, which I doubt, he would certainly have signed his own first name. I think you had better uncover more evidence. To work!" *Turn to 405.*

You study the groom for a moment. "You know, Oliver, a lot of people were surprised that Irish Star ran so badly today. Colonel Stuart thinks something was done to the horse. Do you have any idea what might have happened or why the horse ran so poorly?"

"Me, guv?" Oliver asks in surprise. "Why, if I knew what made a horse run good some days and bad others, I'd be making a better living than I gets for mucking out stables. Even the best horse is unpredictable as the weather. Why, there's men what say there's fifty ways a horse can lose a race, or more! So the Colonel's just grasping at straws when he claims that somethin' was done to the horse." Rocking on his heels, Oliver pauses, expecting a reply.

- *If you say nothing,* **turn to 666.**
- *If you ask how Irish Star trained,* **turn to 272.**

496

"Did you see anything unusual in the lounge when you brought the note to Colonel Sylvester?" you ask. "Did he react when you gave him the note?"

The solicitor stops to think a moment, then nods. "You ask someone not bound by the Club rules, eh?" he laughs, then goes on. "I came to the club, and the doorman told me where the Colonel sat, placing great emphasis on the club rule of absolute silence."

"What happened then?" you ask.

"I followed the butler to the lounge, and he pointed out Colonel Sylvester to me. I walked over to him and stood waiting for him to look up. He rather pointedly ignored me."

"The Colonel was ever a stickler for the rules," Sir Andrew mutters, and you wave him to silence.

"Yes, well, after a moment," Hamilton continues, "I dropped the note in his lap, from which it fell to the floor. Then I turned and walked away, as I did not expect or desire a reply. Just as I reached the door, I heard the thud of something falling. The Colonel was sprawled out on the floor, and the first man to touch him said he was dead. He had the envelope in his hand, but it looked to me as if he had not opened it." **Turn to 245.**

497

"What did you think of Colonel Sylvester?" you ask Hamilton.

"Think of him?" Hamilton answers in a questioning tone. "Why, I did not know the man at all, or anything about him."

- *If you ask him why he wrote the note,* **turn to 417.**
- *If you repeat the question,* **turn to 333.**

498

"A list of my clients?" Amber asks, shocked. "I would not insult them by writing their names into a book!" **Turn to 528.**

499

"Thank you, Sir Andrew," you say with deep respect. "You've been most helpful." *Turn to 475.*

500

You hastily tell your audience that Oliver had possession of the drug and that he received a large payment from Roscoe, who had no apparent reason to give him money.

Watson cries "Bravo!" in delight at your success, although you receive as much satisfaction from Mr. Holmes' curt nod of approval.

"Very nice," the detective says, covering the most important points. "You are beginning to show signs of common sense." *Turn to 460.*

501

Watson expresses his shock when you explain the coded message.

"My word, Holmes!" he exclaims."What a nerve this Hamilton chap has! He himself carries a note to the man, threatening his life, and then he finds some way to do the poor soul in."

"Very daring, indeed," Holmes agrees, "and if we had Mr. Hamilton here I might congratulate him on his nerve, if not his cleverness. Still, while this points to the man, it hardly answers every question. We do not know how he caused Colonel Sylvester's death, if he caused it, nor do we know why."

"Do you have any ideas?" you ask.

"Ideas?" Holmes queries. "That might seem to be an admission that I am investigating the affair, not you. Still," he adds, "I would say that you have two choices. You might continue a straightforward investigation of the facts until you have a more complete case, or you could go to Hamilton, and see if you can bluff him into admitting his guilt. However, if you choose the latter course of action, you had better take Watson and his revolver along..."

"Indeed, he had better," Watson adds warmly.

"Yes, the man might be dangerous," Holmes mutters.

●*If you investigate more fully,* **turn to 584.**
●*If you confront Hamilton,* **turn to 364.**

502

"Henry Hamilton, the solicitor, murdered Colonel Sylvester," you say confidently.

Holmes raises an eyebrow. "Oh?" he asks. "Why do you think he did it?" *Turn to 109.*

"Well, if the Colonel hired you, I suppose I can spare you a moment," the jockey says. "Though I don't know what there is to talk about. The horse ran bad and got its tail whipped. I just take what the trainer gives me and ride it as best I can."

●*If you checked Clue A, turn to 594.*
●*Otherwise, turn to 321.*

504

"You probably know little of Colonel Sylvester," Sir Andrew says, and you nod. "There is little enough to tell, actually. He served in India for some years, then retired from the army and returned to England. He has been in business for the dozen or so years since he returned." *Turn to 434.*

505

You give the letters back to the Valet, and he throws them aside. "If there is anything else I can do for you?" he asks.

●*If you ask to see Sylvester's brandy, **turn to 400.***
●*Otherwise, **turn to 457.***

506

"Lord Hampton was responsible for Oliver's actions," you tell the men. "He wanted to buy the horse, and its defeat lowered the selling price. Also, he had the drug." You await Mr. Holmes' attack upon your logic.

Instead, Dr. Watson smacks his hands together in delight, and even Holmes smiles slightly.

"Very well done," says the detective. "That is quite enough to settle the matter, although it would have been a wiser to prove that no other suspect could have gotten his hands upon the potion. Now, help me decide how to deal with his Lordship, who should be here in a few minutes."

●*If you want to try to solve the mystery again without being given the solution, **turn to the Prologue** and begin anew.*

●*Otherwise, turn to 185.*

507

"Mr. Holmes can be overwhelming," you say in agreement, "and I hope I don't sound too much like him." Roscoe's eyes narrow for just a second, as though expecting something unpleasant. "It's just this," you continue. "When Dr. Watson and I approached, we saw you collecting from   other gentlemen of your profession. That surprised me — I didn't know that you placed wagers with your competitors." **Pick a number** and add your Communication bonus:

- •*If 2-8,* **turn to 486.**
- •*If 9-12,* **turn to 529.**

508

Watson appears to be watching Irish Star with great care, perhaps hoping to notice some flaw that will prove the wisdom of his choice.

"Why, the jockey's feeding something to Irish Star," he suddenly says in surprise. "This is a funny time for that, I should think." **Check Clue A. Turn to 408.**

509

The pudgy Admiral enters with the most dignified waddle you have ever seen. He is a huge, portly man of three hundred pounds, and the rolling gait produced by a lifetime at sea is accentuated by his great bulk. He greets you cheerfully, assuring you that his long wait has been no problem.

- •*If you ask him what he saw,* **turn to 449.**
- •*Otherwise,* **turn to 605.**

510

"The dastardly villain," says Watson. **Turn to 999.**

511

"Did you and your late cousin get along well?" you ask Colonel Stuart.

"My cousin did not like anybody," Stuart says sharply. "And being a man of some taste and judgment, I avoided his company whenever possible." **Turn to 462.**

512

"Why, he must be writing an adventure," you say. "That's just what the pile of manuscript at his elbow appears to be. And if he didn't like what he was writing, he'd just crumple the sheet and drop it. Besides, letters would not occupy his mind as fully. Finally, I would expect to see a pile of finished letters in envelopes."

Holmes smiles. "Very good. Now see if you know what he was writing about." **Turn to 283.**

513

A more thorough search of the stable reveals nothing of interest.

•*If you search elsewhere, turn to 105.*
•*Otherwise, turn to 298.*

514

"Henry Raines must be the guilty man," you say, trying to sound confident.

Holmes shakes his head. "There's not a shred of evidence pointing to him," replies the detective, "and in addition, a man with his position in the racing world would not risk it all by intentionally losing one race. The profit could never be worth the gamble."

•*If you want to try to solve the mystery again without being given the solution, turn to the Prologue and begin anew.*

•Otherwise, *turn to 294.*

515

"Now, Mr. Oliver," you say, studying him, "I know you can give me a better answer than you have. What didn't you like about the way Irish Star behaved before the race?"

"I couldn't hardly say; just odd things here and there. Like he weren't so perky as sometimes. With a horse you knows, you feels things a lot that you can't put into words." *Pick a number and add your Intuition bonus:*

•*If 2-8, turn to 641.*
•*If 9-12, turn to 339.*

516

"I hesitate to consider that a former employer would be a murderer," you say, "but do you have any information on Colonel Staurt?'

"Don't let sentiment muddle an investigation," snaps Holmes. "Why, even if Watson should take the path of crime, he knows that I would not let our friendship stop me from pursuing him." Your cousin's smile at this jibe is a little forced.

Holmes searches his shelves, then pulls down a volume. "This might help," he says. "It's published for the horse racing business and describes the background of many of those who own and race horses. They are most concerned about the integrity of those who race, since the damage from a scandal would be so great."

You read the paragraph about Stuart. When in the service, he spent some time as a subaltern in India, but passed most of his career commanding an outpost in the West Indies. You comment on this.

"Yes," Holmes agrees, "not an exciting history for a man who so fits the image of a fighting officer. But Colonel Stuart is not a rich man, and a lower prestige regiment assigned to the islands would give him a better opportunity to rise in rank. That is probably the only way he was able to achieve field rank." *Check Deduction 16. Turn to 413.*

517

You cannot remember having read about the chemical properties of this particular drug.

●*If you have Clue G, turn to 601.*
●*Otherwise, turn to 302.*

518

You find it a little surprising that Sylvester received such long letters from the employees of his rivals. The letters don't seem as succinct as ordinary business writing. Then, on a hunch, you apply the secret code to the letters. Translated, they reveal that the letters gave Sylvester information ruinous to his rivals. Armand is one of the victims.

"This explains one thing," you say to Watson. "The envelope as well as the note was in code, and the 13 in the corner must be some kind of signal for a coded message. As soon as Sylvester saw it on that fateful day at the Diogenes Club, he knew that someone had broken his code, and therefore probably had the means to ruin him. Naturally, he drained his brandy at a gulp, and it did its work on him." *Turn to 505.*

519

Delighted at having figured out the code, you relish the key clue.
Follow the instructions in the next paragraph, written in the same code, until they direct you where to turn. If you do not know the code, turn to 438.

To quite quickly read the secret code, you must take your time. First, find key word; second, count every word; and third, skip alternating word that comes thereafter. From this, turn notes around to see that 235 is dummy paragraph, and you turn instead to paragraph 316.

Watson looks a bit perplexed by Holmes' rejection of your reasoning. "Well, Holmes," he asks gruffly, "if my cousin is wrong, then how was Colonel Sylvester killed?"

"I know how, Watson," Holmes replies, "but I want to clarify one or two more details before I explain it to the pair of you. Wait here; I shan't be more than an hour."

You and Dr. Watson fidgit and debate the case until you hear the door to Baker Street swing open and slam shut. Holmes returns within the hour, a satisfied look in his eyes.

"Well, do you know everything now?" Watson demands in a somewhat peevish tone of voice.

"Knowing everything is a bold claim for anybody to make Watson, but I know enough," the detective answers. "I have just spoken to Mr. Grable at Henry Hamilton's former law offices, and what he told me provided the motive. I already knew that he was the killer, from the note which he delivered."

"What do you mean?" Watson asks in astonishment. "What about the note?"

"My dear Watson, the note was in code," Holmes patiently explains. "I had little trouble in translating it. In it, Hamilton told Sylvester that he would kill him. When Sylvester bent over to pick up the note, Hamilton dropped the drug in his drink, then turned away. As soon as Sylvester saw the envelope, also written in code, the shock caused him to drain his glass, which brought on the fatal stroke."

"But why, Holmes?" you demand.

The detective sighs. "That is what I learned from Grable. A military blunder by Colonel Sylvester caused the death of Hamilton's brother-in-law in a most horrible manner. When she learned of how her brother died, Hamilton's wife suffered a total breakdown. They went out to Nassau because the doctors said that was the only hope for her. She apparently suffered for years and finally died last year. Hamilton returned to England to avenge her suffering and the damage to his own career caused by the long exile." *Turn to 546.*

521

You learn nothing more. *Turn to 999.*

522

"Very good," Holmes says, "a confession makes matters easier. Good work." His praise warms your heart. *Turn to 460.*

523

You see two men just joining the crowd, one dressed nattily, like an upper class dandy, and the other wearing the loud clothes of the lower type of sporting toff. "What's wrong with them, Mr. Holmes?" you ask.

Holmes looks at you with approval. "You're learning," he mutters. *Turn to 142.*

524

Oliver flushes angrily, and you brace yourself for trouble. "You ask too many questions, snoop!" he screams, springing toward you with his fists raised. *Pick a number and add your Athletics bonus.*

- •If 2-6, *turn to 542.*
- •If 7-12, *turn to 227.*

525

You begin your explanation by translating the coded note to Holmes and go on to tell him about the other evidence you have uncovered.

- •*If you checked Deduction 23, or Deductions 17, 18 and 19, turn to 192.*
- •*If you checked Clue R and Deduction 17, turn to 533.*
- •*Otherwise, turn to 115.*

526

"There's nothing but brandy in this sample, Mr. Holmes," you say, pleased when he nods in agreement.

- •*If you checked Clue O, turn to 264.*
- •*Otherwise, turn to 393.*

527

As various people collect money from Roscoe and the clerk, you notice that the clerk puts a mark on a sheet of paper every time someone is paid. You guess that it must be a list of those who wagered on the race.

- •*If you try to look at the list, turn to 414.*
- •*Otherwise, turn to 586.*

528

Having all the information from Amber's you dare to expect, you thank him for his time and leave. *Turn to 614.*

529

"Oh, that would be strange to a man not familiar with my trade," Roscoe says, laughing his booming laugh again. "We call the practice of wagering amongst ourselves 'laying off.' When I gets too much action on one horse, especially a long shot, I places some of it with me rivals, in order to lessen the danger. That way you avoid making a huge payoff when the occasional longshot comes in. I'm especially suspicious cause Lord 'ampton had a long shot running, as I didn't much care for the favorite. All this lovely money you saw me get will disappear as my customers come around. You'll see. Watch!" *Turn to 293.*

530

Colonel Stuart appears ready to bite your head off at the question, then smiles and blushes. "I needed money very badly," he explains. "When you dealt with me before, I believe you learned that I was — I am — financially ailing, shall we say? Because I despised him, I had sworn that I would never ask my cousin for money, but at last, I reached a stage where others would be hurt as well as myself. So I came here and gave the waiter at the bar a note for him. Then I waited in the Strangers' Room for him to come. Instead, Sir Andrew came with word that my cousin was dead." *Check Clue B. Turn to 171.*

531

You explain how the clues fit together, as both Holmes and Watson listen closely.

●*If you checked Deduction 23, or Deductions 17, 18 and 19,* ***turn to 192.***

●*If you checked Deductions 17 and 18,* ***turn to 131.***
●*If you checked Clue R and Deduction 17,* ***turn to 446.***
●*Otherwise,* ***turn to 490.***

532

You trade a few pleasantries with Armand, then suddenly ask: "What can you tell us about Sunflight?"

"Sunflight?" he answers, obviously mystified by the word. "What is Sunflight — a new brandy you desire me to import?" *Turn to 187.*

533

Holmes listens to your explanation and nods in satisfaction. "You present a sound and sensible solution to the case," he says, "although it is always possible to do better. The note shows that Hamilton hated Sylvester enough to kill him, and you have shown that Hamilton had the West Indian background necessary to have committed the crime. You could have made a stronger case if you had discovered physical evidence regarding Hamilton's motive for despising Sylvester." *Turn to 539.*

534

You test the brandy sample from Colonel Sylvester's bottle. *Pick a number and add your Scholarship bonus:*

- *If 2-7, turn to 301.*
- *If 8-12, turn to 193.*

535

"A list of my clients?" Amber asks. "But why?"

"If any known enemy of the Colonel's bought this brandy," you patiently explain, "it might indicate that he substituted a poisoned bottle. I hardly expect to find anything," you add hastily, seeing the doubt in his eyes. "I merely hope to eliminate a possibility."

With this explanation, he furnishes a brief list of names. Except for Sylvester's, none of the names is familiar. *Turn to 528.*

536

"Opinion!" he snaps, "what do you mean, opinion? I joined this club so that I need not have opinions of the men around me." *Turn to 560.*

537

"I met Colonel Sylvester once or twice," Hamilton explains. "When involved in business transactions, he tended to avoid payments unless they were forced upon him. I represented one or two people who needed legal assistance to seek and receive remedy. From them, and via preliminary research into the case, I came to the conclusion that the gallant colonel was a greedy and unscrupulous man." A coughing fit overtakes the solicitor, and several moments of silence ensue until he regains his speech. "Excuse me. I assure you that I barely knew him, and I had no desire to know him better." *Turn to 411.*

538

You mingle a little with the crowd, then stop near the two men, your interest apparently held by your program.

"So Colonel Stuart's debts to you are overdue too, Bench?" Phillips asks the smith.

"To me and every other man on the grounds!" the smith growls. "I don't like to say so, cause he's a great sportsman and good for the game, but if Irish Star doesn't bring him a purse today, I think we all will have to speak to the stewards. The Colonel may have to sell Irish Star, I reckon, but I have babes to feed, and so do all the others."

Phillips nods heavily. "I'll go along then," he agrees. "But I think Stuart has the money. Irish Star is the best horse in the race, and I hear he's been training very well indeed." As you turn away from the conversation, you notice your friends returning. *Check Clue B. Turn to 358.*

539

Although you have correctly named the murderer, you have not obtained all the evidence incriminating Hamilton. Perhaps you should return to the beginning of the case and see if you can present Mr. Holmes with a complete solution, explaining Motive, Method, and Opportunity.

•*If you begin again, turn to 237.*
•*If you want to hear Holmes' complete explanation, turn to 520.*
•*If you want to pursue the killer, turn to 546.*

540

"An odd deduction," sneers Holmes. *Turn to 999.*

541

You and Watson have no idea where Hamilton has gone. You can find no way to pursue him further at this moment. *Turn to 409.*

542

You regain consciousness to find Oliver splashing water on you. "Sorry to whip you like that, guv," he says, helping you stand, "but I couldn't let no man call me no liar, now could I?" Hardly feeling like going another round with the heavy-fisted groom, you say nothing. *Turn to 641.*

543

A steward ushers in the Honourable Charles Martin, and you immediately form the impression of a man who is always careful, prepares himself immaculately, and presents exactly the appearance he wishes others to see. He is dressed with the utmost neatness and style, without a hint of flashiness, and his movements are precise.

•*If you ask what he saw in the lounge,* **turn to 233.**
•*Otherwise,* **turn to 550.**

544

You regain consciousness outside the flat, with Watson ministering to your bruises. When you ask why he didn't force some answers from the valet, he explains that the valet threatened to summon the police if Watson didn't take you away at once. Since you had picked the lock to get in, Watson did not dare force the question. You realize that this visit was not one of your better efforts. *Turn to 457.*

545

Breathing heavily, Roscoe lies dazed and bruised at your feet, his shocked clerk trying to revive him.

•*If you read the list,* **turn to 116.**
•*If you question Roscoe,* **turn to 397.**

546

You anxiously await any further suggestions Holmes might have.

•*If you checked Clue Q,* **turn to 555.**
•*Otherwise,* **turn to 554.**

547

"Mr. Holmes," you begin, "do you have anything in your records on Colonel Sylvester? If I knew more about him, it might be easier to discover who killed him and why."

Holmes nods. "I took some notes and clippings about him and put them in my commonplace books," he explains. "I thought that he was a man who might enter my line of business some day. I rather expected him to be a criminal rather than a victim," he rather morosely adds.

Eagerly, you read the material. Sylvester had left the army, apparently in some disgrace, although Holmes does not know the details. Back in England, he had engaged in a number of business speculations, dealing in cloth, spirits and lumber. His reputation for an unscrupulous ruthlessness was born out by several of the clippings. He often strayed close to law-breaking and seemed to delight in the ruin of his competitors, both domestic and foreign. One Frenchman, for example, had been reduced from great wealth to running a very small business in wine and spirits.

"That isn't all," Holmes adds, "there were many others ruined just as he ruined this Frenchman, Pierre Armand."

Watson looks up in surprise. "Pierre Armand, Holmes?" he asks. "Why, he is listed as staying in the Royal William Hotel, down near the docks." *Check Deduction 14.*

•*If you ask Holmes about Armand, **turn to 407.***
•*If not, **turn to 305.***

548

Searching your memory of crime news, you remember the name 'Roscoe.' There had been reports in the sporting press that he had unusual luck in anticipating the failure of some highly-touted horses and made large profits as a result. All the evidence indicated, however, that his profits came from purchasing information from stable employees rather than from actually fixing a race. *Turn to 363.*

549

Shocked at the valet's destruction of possible evidence, you jump him, struggling to force him to the floor. *Pick a number and add your Athletics bonus:*

•*If 2-6, **turn to 544.***
•*If 7-12, **turn to 368.***

550

You try to think of the right questions to ask, hoping to get some useful information from this important man.

•*If you ask Martin his opinion of Sylvester, **turn to 643.***
•*Otherwise, **turn to 355.***

551

At a nearby table, you see a man who is slowly drinking himself into a stupor. A black bag rests on the table beside him, and from the teasing of people who speak to him, you realize that he is a veterinarian.

• *If you ask him about the drug,* **turn to 137.**
• *Otherwise,* **turn to 480.**

552

Holmes shakes his head, obviously disappointed, as you answer the question. "No, no," he says, "how can you fail to point the finger where it belongs?"

• *If you want to try again,* **turn to the Prologue** *and begin anew.*
• *Otherwise,* **turn to 156.**

553

"Did you get along well with your cousin?" you ask.

Stuart looks a little surprised, then nods. "Well, that's a fair question I guess, as he died so suddenly. We did not get along well, I'm afraid, though I was his only close relation. He was a hard-natured man who neither liked nor trusted anyone; he probably felt that they were all talking about him behind his back. And there was little to like or respect about him — he was a coward and a fool when he was in India, and a cheating, dishonest businessman since he returned to England. When I made some effort to get along, he showed his dislike, and then described to me in detail his insulting will."

"What about his will?" you ask, stifling your surprise.

"Why, he almost accused me of wanting to murder him," the man continues, his indignation showing. "In the will, it specifies that I will not inherit a penny if he dies in any suspicious manner, not until someone else is proved guilty. If I weren't in such desperate financial straits, I should have told him to leave his fortune to his cat!" *Check Clue B. Turn to 462.*

554

"You were not able to read the coded message in the note that Hamilton brought to Colonel Sylvester," Holmes says, "and that note seals the solicitor's guilt."

"What was the code, Holmes?" Watson demands. "How could a

simple note condemn a man?"

Holmes face assumes an expression of stone, that of the eager hunter. "It was a simple code, Watson. The first word and every third word thereafter formed the real message. I recognized it as soon as I looked at the envelope, because the Colonel's initials are wrong, as was the address of the Club. The number 13 at the top of both letter and envelope is a strong indication that something is hidden in the note. The translated message reads: 'My life is pain from your disgrace. It cost me my love. The price your immediate death. Henry Hamilton.'"

"By jove, Holmes, it's as good as a confession,"exclaims Dr. Watson. *Turn to 555.*

555

"Hamilton remains free," Holmes says, "but I trust that he has not fled yet. I doubt that he will attempt an escape until he knows someone suspects him."

The detective turns to you and gives you a note. "Take this to Hamilton. It tells him, in code, that we know of his guilt. That should drive him to either confession or flight."

"I'll go right now, Holmes," you say eagerly.

The detective slows you with a gesture. "Watson," he commands, "please accompany your cousin, in case he needs help. Take your revolver — murderers are murderers, after all."

Watson nods, and the pair of you hurry off in a hansom, Holmes' last words ringing in your ears.

"Go quickly! The game is afoot!" *Turn to 210.*

556

You arrive at the Royal William Hotel, a small, comfortable place near the Thames. After you send up your cards, Armand comes down to meet you in a small lounge.

You find him a very typical Frenchman, with a round face broken by a neat black mustache. "What can I do for you, gentlemen?" he asks.

●*If you checked Clue R and Deduction 15, turn to 425.*
●*Otherwise, turn to 187.*

557

"Saw, sir?" the waiter replies, a little puzzled. "Well, I didn't hardly see nothing. I just took the gentlemen their drinks. It was like it always is here at this club, all the men just sit and read and never say a thing. Most pleasant, I find it, not like some clubs where 'alf the members want to pretend they's your mate."

"How many drinks did Colonel Sylvester have?" you ask.

"The Colonel had two, sir. I remarked on it, for it was unusual for him. He generally just had the one glass while he was reading his paper." *Turn to 246.*

558

You and Watson enter the storeroom of a grocer, and searching carefully, find no sign of anyone hiding. A word with the storekeeper reveals that no one has run through this shop. *Turn to 567.*

559

"What do you think was the purpose of the note?" you ask Hamilton anxiously. "What gives it that odd quality you mentioned?"

"I cannot put my finger on it," he says slowly, hesitantly. "But the way it is written is bizarre. Something is wrong with some of the words and how they are put together."

●*If you ask him if he thinks the writer was a foreigner,* **turn to 299.**
●*Otherwise,* **turn to 401.**

560

You thank Lord Trent for his time and cooperation. "Hardly had a choice, did I?' he answers with a smile. "Good evening." *Turn to 168.*

561

The second building has no back door, but its cellar doors open on the alley. You and Watson slip cautiously down the steps and find yourself amidst the casks and barrels of a wine merchant. Careful searching shows that Hamilton is not hiding here. You walk up the inner stairs to the store, and after you explain your presence, the owner tells you that no one has run through there. *Turn to 567.*

562

"But why did you bet on Irish Star, if you knew he was running poorly?" you inquire."Colonel Stuart saw you place the bet himself."

"Twere only half a crown, Guv," he answers quickly. "And like you said, the master were there. If I'd bet any other way, it would have cost me my job, and maybe a whipping on top of it." *Pick a number and add your Intuition bonus:*

●*If 2-8,* **turn to 641.**
●*If 9-12,* **turn to 339.**

"What do you mean, Mr. Holmes?" you ask, startled. "What men?"

"Those two men there," he says, and points out two men in the crowd. One is dressed in the elegance of the upper classes, while the other wears the loud clothes of the sporting toff. *Turn to 142.*

You find the offices of Barnes, Grable and Anderson, where Henry Hamilton was once a junior associate, in a solid stone building near the Old Bailey. The office fittings, furniture, drapes and lights are very solid and reliable. This is obviously the sort of conservative old firm that is the bulwark of the Empire.

After a wait of thirty minutes, you go in to see George Grable, the senior partner in the firm. Old and thin, he seems fragile, but his eyes are still sharp and cunning. "What may I do for you, gentlemen?" he asks pleasantly.

"I am seeking some information on one of your former associates, Mr. Henry Hamilton," you explain.

"Information?" he asks in surprise. "For what purpose, sir? We don't discuss our colleagues to pass the time of day."

•*If you explain that Hamilton might be connected with a suspicious death,* **turn to 291.**

•*If you say you might hire Hamilton,* **turn to 636.**

Colonel Stuart leads the way through the crowd and around the stands to the stable area. He strides briskly, forcefully, and people seem to scurry out of his way. *Turn to 174.*

"Of course!" you suddenly exclaim. "The race entries are always on the back page. One of my friends looks them up every day. And if the thought of race entries distracted my cousin, he m . st be writing about a case involving horse racing. I assume this Silver Blaze you mentioned must be a race horse you were involved with at some time."

Watson laughs and applauds. "He will challenge you any day now, Holmes," he says. "Though I'm not sure I like the idea of two of you reading volumes from my every gesture."

Holmes nods in more restrained praise. "It will do for a start," he admits. *Turn to 442.*

567

You and Watson emerge into the main street, but there is no sign of the fugitive. Fortunately, Watson spots one of Holmes' irregulars, who tells you he saw a man like Hamilton hurry away in a hansom just a moment ago. *Pick a number.*

• *If 2-7, turn to 541.*
• *If 8-12, turn to 468.*

568

"Lord Trent," you continue, trying to be as respectful as possible, "what was your opinion of Colonel Sylvester?"

He stares back at you, surprised for a moment. *Pick a number and add your Communication bonus:*

• *If 2-4, turn to 536.*
• *If 5-7, turn to 220.*
• *If 8-12, turn to 669.*

569

As he paces back and forth, having told his sad story, Hamilton suddenly turns and leaps toward one of the side windows. Having anticipated this, you move to block his escape. *Pick a number and add your Athletics bonus:*

• *If 2-6, turn to 328.*
• *If 7-12, turn to 329.*

570

Colonel Stuart approaches after you finish talking with Raines.

"I trust you have all the information my men can give you," he says. "Is there anything else you wish to do in the stable? I have an appointment. "

• *If you ask to search the stables, turn to 172.*
• *Otherwise, turn to 298.*

571

You explain that Oliver had possession of the drug, and therefore almost had to be the one who drugged the horse. Holmes nods in agreement. "You are learning," he says slowly. "It's a good case, although you require assistance in determining who put Oliver up to it, correct?"

Solemnly, you nod.

• *If you want to try to solve the mystery again without being given the solution, turn to the Prologue and begin anew.*
• *Otherwise, turn to 460.*

572

"Is there anything about Oliver's recent behavior that would cause one any concern?" you ask.

"What do you mean?" replies Colonel Stuart. "That is your task to discover! Or do you think I had something to do with my horse losing?" You hurriedly assure him that the thought has never entered your mind. *Turn to 481.*

573

Watson's fidgeting distracts you at the wrong moment, and Hamilton gets a start on you as he dashes across the street, calling for a cab. *Pick a number and add your Athltics bonus:*

• *If 2-10, turn to 635.*
• *If 11-12, turn to 141.*

574

Trying to pick out key details from Watson's desk, you note envelopes, stamps and spare pens in the various slots along the raised back. A pile of papers rests at the left side, while the good doctor pretends to write, perhaps to help you in your observations. *Turn to 435.*

575

"Who might have killed Colonel Sylvester?" you ask Mycroft.

He pauses to think for several moments, then replies: "I cannot name a suspect, but I can offer several plausible motives. Sylvester was a sharp dealer in business, and delighted in upsetting others with letters to the press and similar activities, but I doubt that such nonsense would prove to be grounds for murder. Not unless he ruined somebody, and I know that did not apply to any of the members who were in the lounge. No," he says, leaning back in the sagging stuffed chair, "you might look back to his military career, for if someone blamed him for some misdeed then, he might yet hold the grudge." *Pick a number and add your Intuition bonus:*

• *If 2-8, turn to 632.*
• *If 10-12, turn to 265.*

576

You wonder whether you can learn anything from Roscoe and his friends.

• *If you seek out Roscoe, turn to 432.*
• *Otherwise, turn to 668.*

577

Your tests work well, although the resulting powder is unfamiliar to you. It is obviously organic, but your chemistry takes you no further.

Then Holmes mutters, "Sunflight," almost to himself, but doesn't give you any explanation. *Check Clue R. Turn to 104.*

578

When Martin pulls his cab up outside the Riverside Station, it appears that you have arrived too late. A plume of smoke disappears up the main line.

Martin tries to ease your disappointment. "'ere now, matey," he begins. "It's not 'opeless just yet, sir. That were just a slow local 'e took, if he went by train. There's an express in 'alf an hour what will pass his train on the way to Bristol. But I been thinkin' a mite, and there's two other things your man might 'ave done. Boat's just left here, going down the river to Greenwich where it meets the big steamers— 'e might 'ave taken that. Or 'e might 'ave 'idden 'imself in that patch of woods over the other side of the tracks. The boat would be a smart trick, you know. 'e appears to 'ead one way and then doubles back the other. If 'e took that, a telegraph to the authorities at Greenwich will nab 'im." You consider your choices. *Pick a number and add your Scholarship bonus:*

- *If 2-8, turn to 581.*
- *If 9-12, turn to 589.*

579

Holmes looks at you in astonishment and disgust as you name the party whom you believe drugged the horse. "No, no," he sighs. "I am grossly disappointed in you."

- *If you want to try again, turn to the Prologue and begin anew.*
- *Otherwise, turn to 148.*

580

You shake your head slowly. "That is not absolutely true, is it?" you ask, trying to phrase it pleasantly.

Hamilton blushes, looks angry, but nods. "It's not something I am proud of," he explains. *Turn to 537.*

581

Though you try to remember anything else useful in this situation, nothing comes to mind. *Turn to 597.*

"Yes, Mr. Holmes," you say, following Watson's comment, "do any of your books tell about his Lordship?"

"Of course they do," Watson interjects. "Holmes has information on every man of any interest in London. It is a major part of his genius."

Holmes smiles thinly at the compliment, then pulls down the requested volume. There is little in it about Lord Trent. "He has lived all his life in London, dealt in railroads extensively, and has a reputation for ruthless but honest business dealings," Holmes summarizes.

•*If you checked Clue Q,* ***turn to 416.***
•*Otherwise,* ***turn to 177.***

You boldly approach Lord Hampton and introduce yourself. After congratulating him on his victory, you explain your job.

"Colonel Stuart was very unhappy with Irish Star's performance and wanted Mr. Holmes to investigate," you say, watching closely Lord Hampton's reactions. "As Mr. Holmes had to catch a train, I inherited the task. I should appreciate the views of a man with as much experience with horses as you have, your lordship."

After looking perplexed for a moment, Lord Hampton nods and leads you to a small, tidy office beside his stable.

"With a subject this delicate, I prefer to talk in private," he explains. "Now, how may I help you?"

•*If you ask him about Irish Star,* ***turn to 362.***
•*Otherwise,* ***turn to 629.***

Finished with the note, you give it to Watson for safekeeping. Then turning to Holmes, you ask: "Do you have time to help me examine the rest of the evidence?" ***Turn to 405.***

"No," Holmes continues, " we can rest assured that John Oliver was paid off by a much more respectable man — Lord Hampton." Watson's eyes widen in shock while Colonel Stuart's face hardens.

"Why did he do it, Holmes?" Watson demands, once past his original astonishment.

"Why does any man commit a crime?" the detective muses. "For the excitement perhaps, the thrill of winning the game."

"But he didn't wager heavily on Maiwand!" you say, confused.

"What did he gain by drugging Irish Star?"

"He felt he would gain Irish Star, the horse itself," Holmes explains. "Lord Hampton had offered to buy him and was refused; with Colonel Stuart losing the purse, his Lordship could buy the beast much more cheaply. The workout Irish Star shared with Queensland was probably the decisive stroke. Then, Lord Hampton realized that Colonel Stuart's horse was as good as his champion, even though his record indicated he was inferior." Holmes pauses to relight his pipe and blow curling blue rings toward the ceiling.

"If Lord Hampton entered his Irish Star in a major stakes at Ascot or Epsom," the detective continues, "he would likely be offered excellent odds, however much he wagered. Last Friday, he bet little because Maiwand was not a certain winner, even with Irish Star eliminated. Last, Lord Hampton was one of the owners who tested Dr. Hastings drug. Now we must deal with him. He should arrive in a few minutes." *Turn to 185.*

586

You bid Dr. Watson a good day as he stuffs his winnings into his pocket and hurries to join Mr. Holmes. "The train!" he calls out to you. *Turn to 228.*

587

You weigh the envelope in your hand.

•*If you read the note,* **turn to 276.**
•*Otherwise,* **turn to 186.**

588

"From the stilted language, I think some foreign enemy of Colonel Sylvester's wrote the note," you say hopefully.

Holmes studies you a moment, then shakes his head in a non-committal way. "If that is the case," he says, "the note cannot be connected to the murder. I suggest you forget it and investigate some other avenue." *Turn to 584.*

589

Holmes' instruction bears fruit. From a boy near the station, you buy a paper that lists ship departures. You turn to the page and find that no ships depart from Greenwich today — taking that boat wouldn't have helped Hamilton. On the other hand, a steamer is supposed to leave Bristol for Nassau at ten o'clock tonight. *Turn to 597.*

You and Watson get off the Express and begin to wander idly around the branch station, even as your train pulls out. The two of you go through the main waiting room with no success and come out on the platform that fronts the branch line.

Suddenly, you hear a cough from around the corner of the station. With Watson, you go to the sound and find Hamilton hiding in the shadows. Hearing your steps, he looks up and momentarily freezes in shock. His fear does not last long, however. He quickly pulls a gun from his pocket, fires a wild shot at you, and dashes across the tracks into the woods. *Pick a number and add your Athletics bonus:*

- *If 2-3,* ***turn to 389.***
- *If 4-12,* ***turn to 646.***

"Bowser and Fitzhugh, the gamblers, drugged the horse," you say. "You pointed them out as they left the stables yourself."

Holmes shakes his head, and the look in his eyes would wither a statue. "No, no," he snaps, "though I wouldn't put the idea past them. They were not there early enough before the race to have done the job. In addition, if they had drugged the horse, they would have wagered far more on the outcome."

•If you want to try to solve the mystery again without being given the solution, ***turn to the Prologue*** *and begin anew.*

•Otherwise, ***turn to 294.***

Carried away by the excitement of the crowd, you pay little attention to the individuals gossiping and learn nothing. ***Turn to 668.***

You ask Sir Andrew to send for Tom Smithson, the waiter.

Smithson soon enters, looking very nervous. He is typical of his type and class, a small, slender man with a most ordinary face, who practically seems to vanish into the background standing there waiting for your questions.

- *If you ask what he saw in the lounge,* ***turn to 282.***
- *Otherwise,* ***turn to 246.***

"I noticed you fed the horse something before the race," you say. "Why was that? I never knew jockeys did anything like that." **Pick a number** and add your Communication bonus:

•*If 2-8, **turn to 232.***
•*If 9-12, **turn to 138.***

595

Sir Andrew reviews his list again. "I should think that it would be best to talk to Mr. Henry Hamilton next. He brought a note to Colonel Sylvester, but had no other connection with the deceased. Do you wish to talk to him?"

•*If you talk to Mr. Hamilton, **turn to 274.***
•*Otherwise, **turn to 334.***

596

"You may have left one name off your interview list," you say to Sir Andrew as he stands.

"What do you mean?" Sir Andrew demands.

"I should like to talk to Tom Smithson, the waiter who served Sylvester the fatal glass of brandy."

Slowly, Sir Andrew nods in reluctant agreement.

•*If you talk to the waiter, **turn to 593.***
•*Otherwise, **turn to 602.***

597

Looking around the train platform, you see that the chief porter is not busy at the moment. You hurry and ask if he saw a man with no luggage board the train for Bristol. **Pick a number** and add your Communication bonus:

•*If 2-7, **turn to 599.***
•*If 8-12, **turn to 604.***

"I hesitate to say such a thing about my own employer," you begin, "but I think Colonel Stuart arranged to have his own horse lose, no doubt to ease his financial problem."

Holmes eyes widen in shock; the Colonel's face reddens and his fists clench threateningly as Watson mutters slowly: "My word, you can't be serious."

"I fear he is, Doctor," Holmes answers, "though how he came up with this solution, one can hardly surmise. When a financially stricken man bets on his own horse, to win, there's hardly reason to believe that he arranged for the horse to lose. Surely you can think more clearly than that! Even Lestrade would do better."

●*If you want to try to solve the mystery again without being given the solution,* **turn to the Prologue** *and begin anew.*

●*Otherwise,* **turn to 585.**

Almost before you can finish your question, the porter shakes his head angrily. "A man with no luggage? What do you think I 'ave, an 'undred eyes or something? I was so busy with that train, I wouldn't have noticed a man with three legs, that I wouldn't." *Turn to 606.*

Holmes glances at you, then asks: "Did you discover what drug was used to slow Irish Star?"

"Yes, Mr. Holmes, I did," you answer, trying to balance your pride and your fear of failure. "It was a compound called *"HASTINGS DISTILLATE OF OPIUM."*

Holmes nods. "Yes, I have heard of that," he says. "It would be an excellent method of slowing a horse, though Dr. Hastings developed it for a much different use."

Colonel Stuart looks sharply at you. "Why, Mr. Holmes, that's remarkable!" he exclaims. "That is just what the track veterinarian found when he examined Irish Star." *Turn to 335.*

You feel a surge of confidence growing within; you have discovered both the man who actually drugged Irish Star and the drug that he used to do it! Surely deducing who paid Oliver to do the job will be a comparatively easy task. **Check Deduction 8.**

●*If you have Oliver arrested,* **turn to 214.**

●*Otherwise,* **turn to 199.**

602

You sigh in relief, pleased that the interviews are completed. The others look almost as pleased.

•*If you checked Decision 20,* **turn to 203.**
•*Otherwise,* **turn to 377.**

603

Holmes fills the rest of your trip to the track with stories from his past investigations, recounting many of the odd sources of information which have yielded clues. You sit drinking it in, hoping you can use some of his ploys when faced with similar problems yourself.

Finally, you reach the Thameside Racing grounds. It is a simple place, for races are run here only a few weeks in the year. Low hills near the track provide alternative seating to the small grandstand and also shield the stables from some of the noise raised by the stands and the nearby railroad. Fresh paint on the stands and fences as well as the excellent condition of the turf show that the groundskeepers have made every effort to get the oval track ready for the races. As you pass through the gates, Holmes glances around him, following his habitual pattern of seemingly observing everything.

"Anything interesting, Holmes?" Watson asks. "I hope we shan't have to give up all these pleasures to pursue some rogue," he laughs.

Holmes smiles thinly. "No rogues, but there's a man who once crossed the line." He indicates a plump little man dressed in tweeds, who is giving directions to a wagon driver. "His name is Phillips. At his wit's end, he was about to steal from an uncle to get the money to go into business. I warned his uncle, who listened to his plans and lent him the money. Now he supplies grain and hay to half the racing stables in the south of England." Suddenly Holmes' face hardens; he mutters, "I'm surprised those men are allowed anywhere near a stable!" *Pick a number and add your Observation bonus:*

- *If 2-8, **turn to 563**.*
- *If 9-12, **turn to 523**.*

604

The porter listens to your question, then nods. "I seen the bloke," he says, "he got on the local a couple minutes before she went off. What do you want him for?"

"He murdered a man," Watson answers, before you can say anything.

"Murdered someone, did he?" The porter thinks a moments. "I'm sure he got on the train, but I'll tell you a dodge some bright lads use to avoid bill collectors and such gentry — they gets on the train from this side and gets off the other. Then they goes and hides in the woods until the man what wants them has gone his way."

You thank the porter and tip him for his information. *Turn to 606.*

605

What questions beg to be asked the Admiral?

- *If you ask his opinion of Sylvester, **turn to 275**.*
- *Otherwise, **turn to 622**.*

606

You realize you must come to a decision — you have all the information you will get in the matter.

"Well, which way shall we go?" asks Watson. "You lead the way and I'll be with you step-for-step."

- *If you think he took the boat, **turn to 139**.*
- *If you search the woods, **turn to 645**.*
- *If you wait for the Express, **turn to 263**.*

Before Hamilton comes in, you explain the coded note to Sir Andrew.

"Are you going to accuse him of the crime then?" he asks.

"I am not certain if I should," you answer. "It is practically a confession, but not absolute proof that he carried out the threat."

Mycroft nods, quietly. "What will you do, then?"

You think about it, then reply: "I will question him. If I decide to accuse him, I will nod sharply, just before I ask him why he wrote the note. If I decide that it is not safe to make the accusation, I shall tap my fingers on the table."

You arrange Sir Andrew and Watson so that all of you will block Hamilton's escape through the door. Then you tell the steward to send Hamilton in.

As he enters, looking drawn and wary, you thank him for his time, offering him a chair. He appears to be a neatly dressed, respectable looking man, neither wealthy nor poor and suffers from a persistent, hacking cough.

"There's no need for thanks," he says. "As a solicitor and an officer of the court, I know it is my duty to provide all possible assistance in a matter of a suspicious death."

"You are most kind, sir," you say. "Now the matter we need your help with is the note you brought to the victim. We know that you were only a messenger, but you have met the man who sent the note, and you are a man of intelligence and education." You hand him the note, and he scans it with a puzzled look.

"It sounds rather odd," he says slowly. "Something not quite right with it."

•*If you ask his opinion of the note,* **turn to 559.**
•*Otherwise,* **turn to 401.**

"Well, did you see anything interesting when you followed Oliver?" you ask the irregular.

"It took some time, guv, but I did finally," Stanly eagerly reports. "He wove here and there through the crowd, but he wasn't looking for a little fellow like me to be following him. And he finally led me to someone else." **Turn to 418.**

Uncertain what to do now, you look to Watson, who gives you an encouraging wink.

●*If you ask the bartender for a sample of Colonel Sylvester's brandy,* **turn to 285.**

●*Otherwise,* **turn to 122.**

610

Colonel Stuart smiles in delight when he sees you, shaking your hand vigorously. "So you're investigating again, are you?" he laughs. "Well, I'm certain you shall solve the matter quickly — if there is anything to be solved." You thank him for the compliment and turn to business.

●*If you checked Deduction 12,* **turn to 423.**

●*Otherwise,* **turn to 326.**

611

You wonder whether any of the others in the lounge had a motive to kill Colonel Sylvester, or to have him poisoned by someone else.

●*If you ask Holmes about motives,* **turn to 615.**

●*Otherwise,* **turn to 620.**

612

By cornering him, you force Hamilton to fight. *Pick a number and add your Athletics bonus:*

●*If 2-8,* **turn to 396.**

●*If 9-12,* **turn to 314.**

613

Together you and Watson deliver the murderer to the police and return in triumph to Baker Street. **Turn to 617.**

614

You consider whom to investigate next.

●*If you checked Deduction 17,* **turn to 450.**

●*Otherwise,* **turn to 158.**

615

"Did any of the others in the lounge have reason to do harm to Colonel Sylvester?" you ask.

"Motive for murder, if murder it was," Holmes mutters. "I have seen some people put up with much more and never lift a hand while others have killed for next to nothing — an imagined slight, a dalliance, whatever. Every man in the room had a motive that might lead him to kill. Of course, this is true of every club in London." *Turn to 620.*

616

"Oh, Tom told you that, did he?" Oliver demands, looking angry. Then he shrugs. "Well, the man has a big mouth, and I believe he likes your Dr. Watson. You see, the horse hadn't run good in his workouts, and if he don't work good, he ain't gonna run good neither. But Tom shouldn't have blabbed."

•*If you have Clue F, turn to 562.*
•*Otherwise, turn to 287.*

617

In response to a telegram from Watson, Holmes has had a delicious supper sent up for the celebration. As you and Watson set to, the great detective smiles sardonically.

"Success tastes sweet, doesn't it?" he says with his dry laugh, "and a most instructive success it was, if I do say so. Though I should think that the Crown might have some little difficulty in proving the man's guilt. He chose his murder 'weapon' with a great deal of care, you must admit."

"Oh there's no difficulty at all in gaining a conviction," Watson answers between mouthfuls. "When we delivered Hamilton to Lestrade, the man gave a full confession. I think he was so shaken by being captured so quickly that he didn't think of the possibilities of his own defense."

"His quick capture was fortunate," Holmes agrees, "for given any time, a murder of this sort would have escaped detection. The man did actually die of a stoke, and I would wager that his doctor had warned Colonel Sylvester of such dangers many a time. Hamilton merely made certain that his victim would die sooner rather than later."

"Aye," Watson agreed, "but I doubt that Hamilton will have a long sentence — he killed because of how his wife suffered after all, not from some more sordid motive."

"Perhaps," Holmes agreed, "but he killed in a ruthless and careful fashion, and I'm sure that he would have killed you two if it would have saved him. Murder is seldom an indication of good character, after all. He took pains to learn Sylvester's weakness, then dropped the note so that the Colonel wouldn't see him drug the brandy. And the note itself was the key to Sylvester's gulping the brandy, so that he got the full dose of the drug in an instant."

"How could that be, Holmes?" Watson asks in his most puzzled tone. "He didn't read the note!"

"The envelope was enough," Holmes answers. "Sylvester knew that anyone else learning his code would lead to his ruin, for such a person could reveal all the Colonel's unethical dealings over the years. And the envelope itself was written in the code! The number 13 in the corner was the indication that the envelope was coded, and that was the discovery that so shocked Colonel Sylvester. For once, the superstitious were proven right, and the number 13 was unlucky indeed."

Though the two friends continue their discussion, their voices seem to fade away. Even as you bask in the glory of this success, you are already beginning to wonder what your next case will be. **The End**

618

Almost before you realize that you are in a fight, Roscoe is driving his fists into your stomach. You fight back desperately, trying to offset his weight advantage. Watson and the clerk keep each other from interfering. *Pick a number and add your Athletics bonus:*

•*If 2-8, turn to 369.*
•*If 9-12, turn to 545.*

619

"Mr. Holmes," you begin, trying to be very formal. "You were in the lounge when Colonel Sylvester died. What did you see at the time? Did anyone approach him?"

Holmes smiles a little. "You are relying upon my talents, friend, but I'm afraid they will do you no good. When here at the club, due to promises I made, I make it a point to see and notice nothing. It is an interesting intellectual exercise to go rigidly against one's in-grained nature and habits." *Turn to 429.*

620

With some relief, you thank Holmes for his patience with your efforts. He too seems to relax. *Turn to 133.*

621

"Well," Holmes sighs, reviewing the evidence, "while Oliver gave the drug to the horse, the man behind the deed is far more important to us. Who was pulling the groom's strings, so to speak?"

•*If you name Colonel Stuart,* **turn to 552.**
•*If you name Lord Hampton,* **turn to 267.**
•*If you name Roscoe,* **turn to 149.**
•*If you name Bowser and Fitzhugh,* **turn to 155.**

622

You thank the Admiral for his help, and the old sailor actually seems disappointed that you do not want to hear more. What a character! **Turn to 596.**

623

"Sir," you begin, "what did you notice regarding Colonel Sylvester's behaviour and actions this afternoon, at the time that you were in the lounge with him?"

He looks down his nose at you as he answers. "One of the reasons I joined this club is a rule that specifically compels us to ignore everyone else. I follow the rule rigidly."

"You noticed nothing?" you repeat.

"Nothing until they asked me to leave the room while they tended to his body. I didn't look at it — dead men are not my idea of hors d'ouvres." **Turn to 180.**

624

Embarassed, you move away. **Turn to 999.**

625

Obviously, the note is a threat from Colonel Stuart to his cousin Colonel Sylvester, although a threat to his wealth rather than his life. **Check Decision 12. Turn to 648.**

626

Lord Trent looks surprised at the question, and you add hurriedly: "I realize that the club rules require that you ignore all that happens around you, but I feel certain it would be difficult to ignore movement at the chair next to yours."

Trent's thin mouth turns up in the faintest of smiles, and he nods. "You are correct; it is almost impossible, especially as there was so much activity that I found it more than a little disturbing.

"Sylvester had a drink brought as soon as he sat down with his paper. Then, a little later, perhaps an hour before he died, a waiter brought him a calling card — that is our customary manner of announcing visitors, as it eliminates the need for talk. The Colonel did not move, and in fact sent for another drink, which was not his custom in the afternoon. Then another man came up to him, turned and left. A few seconds after that the Colonel stood up suddenly, grabbed his glass and drained it — a shocking way to treat good brandy — and fell down. I felt it legitimate to stretch the rules and check his pulse, but he was already dead." *Turn to 303.*

627

You sleep poorly that night, turning the facts of Colonel Sylvester's strange death over and over in your mind. You are grateful that Holmes extended an invitation to consult with him, and you arrive at Baker Street just as Holmes and Watson finish their breakfast.

Both men greet you warmly; Watson is in the mood to tease you a little.

"Well," he asks, smiling, "have you decided whether the unfortunate Colonel was a murder victim yet? Perhaps you shall break some of Holmes' records for speed."

"Now, Watson," Holmes interjects, smiling, "give him a chance. He probably has not analyzed the key evidence yet. For example, he may not have read the note that was found on the body."

●*If you have checked Decision 22,* **turn to 357.**
●*Otherwise,* **turn to 479.**

628

A handwritten label reads: *"HASTINGS DISTILLATE OF OPIUM."* **Check Clue H. Pick a number** and add your *Scholarship bonus:*

●*If 2-6,* **turn to 517.**
●*If 7-9,* **turn to 352.**
●*If 10-12,* **turn to 159.**

629

"I shall be glad to see this matter cleared up," Lord Hampton says, speaking deliberately. "Any hint of scandal is bad for all of us. And it's doubly revolting to see a horse as fine as Irish Star perform so poorly."

•*If you have Clue U,* **turn to 111.**
•*Otherwise,* **pick a number,** *and add your Intuition bonus.*
  •*If 2-6,* **turn to 317.**
  •*If 7-12,* **turn to 178.**

630

"What happened?" Watson demands, as soon as you revive enough to make sense.

"Hamilton and I had a little go with our fists, and he was tougher," you explain sheepishly. "How long was I out?"

"Too long, I'm afraid. I waited upstairs nigh on half an hour before I grew anxious and came down to find you." You sigh in dismay — Hamilton must be long gone now. *Turn to 409.*

631

"What happened?" Watson demands, as soon as you revive enough to make sense.

"Hamilton and I had a little go with our fists, and he was tougher," you explain sheepishly. "How long was I out?"

"Not long. I thought I heard an odd noise down here, and was worried. So I came straight down and found you napping."

The news brings you leaping to your feet. "Then let's be off," you snap, "there may still be time to catch the man." *Turn to 567.*

632

With no other questions to ask him, you thank Mycroft for his assistance. He answers with a solemn nod. Will that chair ever be the same, you wonder. *Turn to 595.*

633

"Could the man have been one of Sylvester's business competitors?" you ask.

"Business?" he asks, as if puzzled, then changes his tone to one of assurance. "Of course, sir, it must have been a business rival! A competitor who gave up all hope of winning could carry out a threat to ruin another man." Then another thought seems to strike him. "But if it was written for that purpose, then it can have nothing to do with his death. I tell you, that is a relief. It is uncomfortable to think that I might have played even an unwitting and minor role in the poor man's death."

- *If you ask why he wrote the note, **turn to 417**.*
- *Otherwise, **turn to 401**.*

634

"Mr. Smith," you ask the steward, "Is there anything special about this brandy of the Colonel's?"

The steward nods. "It's a rare brand, for the monastery does not bottle much. Only one dealer in London, Amber's, imports it. He specializes in rare drinks—many of the members here deal with him, to get what they crave." ***Check Clue M. Turn to 609.***

635

Having fallen, you rise from the dirt of the road to see Hamilton swinging onto a hansom that is already moving away. As you shake off the shock of the fall, it turns a corner and vanishes from sight. While you consider a new course of action, Watson starts waving his hand at an urchin who had been laughing at your distress.

"Why, it's the doctor!" the boy exclaims. "'ow's Mr. 'olmes sir?'"

"Holmes is fine, boy," Watson answers. "But I have no time for talk. Can you find where that cab went?"

"I could given time, sir," he answers, "but you might do better waiting 'ere. The bloke what drives that cab often comes back to pick up riders 'ere. 'e's sweet on one of the girls at the pub on the corner." ***Pick a number.***

- *If 2-7, **turn to 541**.*
- *If 8-12, **turn to 468**.*

636

"I need a solicitor," you explain, "and as I recently met Mr. Hamilton, I was considering him for the task. Before offering him the position, I read his background in a directory. I was curious as to why he suddenly left a major firm like yours to take a colonial post with no chance of advancement. I want a sound man for my affairs, naturally."

The old gent sighs, thinks for a moment, then nods. "I can understand that it would look very peculiar, but actually the details reflect very well on poor Hamilton." He pauses but goes on when he sees that what he has said isn't enough to satisfy you. "Hamilton was a most promising young man, with a good future in his profession and a lovely young wife who would help him reach his best.

"Then tragedy struck. His wife's health was shattered when her brother died tragically, and the doctors insisted that her only chance for recovery lay in moving to a more comfortable climate, where both the change of climate and the change of scene would help to rebuild her shattered constitution. Being the man he is, Hamilton immediately resigned his position with us and went out to the Bahamas. Our head of chambers was able to arrange the post for him. Alas, the poor girl never fully recovered, though apparently the climate did help her. When she died last winter, Hamilton returned to London to try to pick up the pieces of his former life. I can assure you that the poor fellow deserves all the success due any good man."

Mr. Grable settles back in his chair, as though he has told you all you would need or expect to know. *Check Deduction 19. Pick a number and add your Communication bonus:*

- *If 2-7, **turn to 459**.*
- *If 8-12, **turn to 451**.*

637

With a cry of despair, the valet leaps at you, surprising you with the suddenness of his attack. ***Pick a number** and add your Athletics bonus:*

- *If 2-7, **turn to 544**.*
- *If 8-12, **turn to 368**.*

638

"Well," you say, trying to put your thoughts into words. "Dr. Watson must have been very preoccupied with what he was writing. I would guess, with his bulldog nature, that once my cousin sits down to write, he stays at it until he has done a full day's work." *Check Clue Z.*

"Very good," Holmes replies. "There is some hope for your ambition." ***Turn to 311.***

639

"I agree with one of Dr. Watson's opinions," you say, and Watson looks surprised. "I think someone tried to incriminate Colonel Stuart, perhaps in the hope that Sylvester would disinherit his cousin."

Holmes' face doesn't change expression. "Well," he finally says, "if that is the case, it can hardly be relevant to the Colonel's death — anyone attempting such a scheme would hardly want Sylvester dead until after the plot had succeeded." *Turn to 584.*

640

You find nothing of interest, even though you have searched with great thoroughness and found several small (but empty) hiding places.

- *If you search another area,* **turn to 105.**
- *Otherwise,* **turn to 298.**

641

Gazing out the open door, you consider further questions for John Oliver.

- *If you ask whom he saw near the stable,* **turn to 262.**
- *Otherwise,* **turn to 309.**

642

"May I ask you a question or two, Colonel?" you begin.

"Of course," he replies.

"Who takes care of your horse?"

"I employ Henry Raines as trainer," says the Colonel. "He is a well-known man in the field and trains horses for several owners. He is one of the most respected men in the field. The heavy work is done by my groom, John Oliver. He's been with me for two years and has been loyal even when I've been a trifle slow with his pay." *Turn to 410.*

643

"What did you think of Colonel Sylvester as a man?" you ask.

"Why, I didn't know him," Martin replies. "His reputation was none too good, or so I've heard, but then, many a man has that sort of problem. One of the joys of this club is that you need not acknowledge your fellow members in any manner — we merely exist in the same area without disturbing each other. It can be very ...restful." *Turn to 355.*

"You know," you say, "I met another man of the name of Oliver today, a man named Tom Oliver. He's a waiter at Dr. Watson's club. Is he a relative?"

"Tom? now why do you bring him up, I wonder?" the groom asks. "Well, it makes no difference — he's my brother. Strange you should meet us both the same day, eh?" *Check Deduction 10.*

•*If you ask what he told his brother about Irish Star,* ***turn to 320.***
•*Otherwise,* ***turn to 495.***

645

You and Watson search the woods near the Riverside Station, thinking that Hamilton has hidden there. The Bristol Express is long gone before you come to the conclusion that you guessed incorrectly, for there is no sign of the murderer in the woods. *Turn to 409.*

646

You instinctively crouch, and Hamilton's bullet sails over your head. Watson looks at you, fear in his eye. Blundering about a wood after an armed murderer is not everybody's cup of tea.

•*If you go into the woods,* ***turn to 236.***
•*If you seek help from the local authorities,* ***turn to 650.***

647

"Mere opinion," snaps Holmes. *Turn to 999.*

648

Finished with the odd note, you hand it to Watson for safekeeping and ponder your next action.

•*If you checked Decision 20,* ***turn to 189.***
•*Otherwise,* ***turn to 203.***

649

"Tom said I talked down Irish Star?" Oliver asks, his mouth wide open in astonishment. "Why, that fool got me advice turned straight around, guv — I told him to bet his all on the horse. I'd never talk down me own master's horse, guv; it'd cost me my job and all chance of getting another one." *Turn to 495.*

650

"This looks like a matter where the police might be a help," you tell Watson. "Let's seek them out."

He agrees, and you find that the local law consists of a single constable who lives near the station. When you tell him that you are pursuing a murderer, he looks doubtful, ready to chase you off. Desperately, you try to persuade him that you are serious. *Pick a number and add your Communication bonus:*

• *If 2-6, turn to 652.*
• *If 7-8, turn to 653.*
• *If 9-12, turn to 655.*

651

"Irish Star is a fine looking horse," Watson admits, studying the handsome gray. But as he runs through a patter of admiration (even though he didn't bet on the horse), it seems to you that Irish Star looks dull and heavy-footed, as if he is sleep- walking. *Turn to 508.*

652

"Murderer, you say," the constable laughs. "You city types take us for fools out here. Murderer, indeed. And me with two chicken thieves I have to chase down. Get out of here."

Hurriedly you and Watson leave. You search the woods yourself, but you have no luck. Eventually, you give up and catch a train for home. *Turn to 409.*

653

After you argue for some time, the constable finally accepts your statement. "Come with me, sir, I'll take you to the magistrate, and he'll take care of the matter."

After the magistrate listens to your story, backed now by the constable, he sends telegrams to the law officers in all the neighboring towns, in the hope that they might catch Hamilton. *Pick a number.*

• *If 2-8, turn to 661.*
• *If 9-12, turn to 660.*

654

For a time, there is little talk, as you wait for the signal that the race results are official. As you stand waiting, a tall, heavy man hurries up to you. He looks like the stereotype of a former Army officer, ramrod-backed, with a red face set off by a greying mustache.

"Mr. Sherlock Holmes?" he asks your companion, and the detective nods. "I thought I recognized you," he says. "I am Colonel Ian Stuart, owner of Irish Star. As you may be aware, he was the heavy favorite for the race today."

"I am aware of that fact," Holmes answers coldly. "I lost a pound on him, as it happens."

"Then if you know racing, sir, you know that something was done to my horse today. I should like you to investigate the matter."

This time, Holmes' chill warms slightly. "I did notice something amiss," he replies. "I will admit that it might be an interesting investigation. However, I must catch a train tonight, and I fear I have no time for any other case until I return." Then he softens, perhaps taking pity at the man's downcast face. "You might try Dr. Watson's cousin here," he adds.

"Do you recommend him, sir?" the Colonel responds.

"He is young at the trade, but he is no more blind and foolish than the police detectives," Holmes answers with no hint of jest. "You could do worse."

When Colonel Stuart offers you the job, you nod eagerly and quickly begin to question him. *Pick a number* and *add your Intuition bonus:*

●*If 2-7, turn to 410.*
●*If 8-12, turn to 642.*

655

The Constable quickly and enthusiastically accepts your explanation. Ready for the chase, he takes you to the local magistrate. Also excited, that gentleman sends telegrams to every surrounding town, then raises a dozen men to enter the wood after Hamilton. *Pick a number.*

●*If 2-5, turn to 661.*
●*If 6-12, turn to 660.*

656

"You make it sound as though the Colonel blundered somehow in his military career," you say. "What events ended his career?"

Mycroft looks pleased. "Sherlock teaches well," Mycroft says to Watson, then turns back to you. "Sylvester might have remained in command for years, if he had not had the misfortune to be sent out on an independent action against a group of marauders. When camped one night, his outposts came under fire. Believing himself besieged by superior numbers, he sent a staff officer and an orderly with an urgent message requesting reinforcements. The rebels caught the pair and tortured them to death. Daylight revealed that there were no more than fifty rebels attacking the camp, and the loss of men by his panic dismayed his superiors. Shortly thereafter, Sylvester was persuaded to retire from military life."

As you take in the implications of the tale, Mycroft sighs, adding: "If you uncover a connection between Sylvester's death and those blunders, then you shall have something." *Turn to 632.*

657

You consider Sir Andrew's description of the waiter.

●*If you ask about Smithson and the Colonel, turn to 673.*
●*Otherwise, turn to 119.*

658

Wondering if further questioning of Mycroft will prove fruitful, you consider asking if he has some idea of who might have murdered Sylvester.

●*If you ask Mycroft who might have killed the Colonel, turn to 575.*
●*Otherwise, turn to 632.*

659

You nod encouraginly towards Colonel Stuart, trying to decide if there's anything more to ask him.

●*If you ask him what happened that day, turn to 230.*
●*Otherwise, turn to 171.*

660

Due to the actions of the magistrate, Hamilton is caught trying to board the southbound train at the next station. You and Watson return to Baker street in triumph. *Turn to 617.*

661

The hunt goes on all night, but you hear no news of Hamilton. He has evidently escaped his pursuers. *Turn to 409.*

662

As you talk, you look around Lord Hampton's small office. *Pick a number and add your Observation bonus:*

●*If 2-8, turn to 165.*
●*If 9-12, turn to 217.*

663

"Of course! " Holmes comments. "I felt something was wrong when I saw how lifeless the horse was when he came out of the gate. Remember what I told you about watching for crimes before they can be committed?"

"Yes, sir," you answer. "Who would have done such a thing? Will you investigate it?"

"I hardly have time, since Watson and I must catch our train in an hour. There are three or four possibilities that come to mind, however."

"What are they?" you ask.

"Surely you saw them for yourself," answers the detective, "but I will detail them for you. That will save Watson the trouble of inventing the dialogue if he writes about this little mishap. I believe I mentioned my surprise at seeing Bowser and Fitzhugh near the stables. Drugging a horse is not beneath them. Second, I have always wondered at Roscoe — he has had some remarkable successes in his day. Then, there are those who would say that Lord Hampton would do almost anything to help one of his horses win — not for the money, but for the thrill of owning a winner. And suppose that Colonel Stuart, Irish Star's owner, has serious financial problems. It would be a clever ploy to put a horse in a race he's too good for and then make sure he loses while backing one of the competition. But only investigation would show which is true, or whether the guilty party, if there is only one, is someone we haven't become aware of. For example, some other horseman might want to buy Irish Star, and the defeat combined with Colonel Stuart's hypothetical financial problems would guarantee a cheaper selling price." *Turn to 654.*

664

You decide not to talk to Holmes. *Turn to 999.*

665

You try to convince the guard that you have business with the stewards. *Pick a number and add your Communication bonus:*
- If 2-7, turn to 540.
- If 8-12, turn to 322.

666

After an awkward pause, Oliver continues. "Yessir, I think it was just a bad day for the horse. Shook me, cause he trained well for the race, but it happens to the best of 'em sometimes." Then he winks. "Before you spends too much time detecting, just remember that the Colonel ain't all that good at paying his bills, right?" *Turn to 641.*

667

"Poppycock," snorts Watson. *Turn to 999.*

668

Checking your watch, you see that it is almost time to meet Holmes' irregular; you must leave the track now. *Turn to 154.*

669

"Opinion!" he says, a faint excuse for a smile crossing his lined face. "My opinion is that if he was murdered, it is hardly a surprise. He was an unkind, ugly man. I cannot say that he did anything illegal in his business, but he certainly strayed close to the line. We were in competition, you understand, and we would take any chance to gain the advantage. He had a sharp mind, as he showed in his letter-writing, and could make the most ridiculous idea seem reasonable, until I dismembered his logic. Still, all-in-all, Sylvester was a bastard of the first water — few people will miss him." *Turn to 560.*

670

Holmes laughs. "You seem to share too many of Watson's good qualities, as befits his cousin. It is a clever murder, and difficult to prove, but murder it was. There can be no doubt." *Turn to 395.*

671

"What was your opinion of Colonel Sylvester?" you ask.

He looks startled. "I don't have an opinion of any of the members, sir — it's not allowed. Only thing I knew of the Colonel was that he commanded my poor brother's regiment."

•*If you ask about his brother, turn to 146.*
•*Otherwise, turn to 269.*

672

Hamilton never hears a sound as you sneak up on him. When close enough, you leap on him, and his gun goes flying. Fighting Hamilton, you have no breath left to call to Watson for help. *Pick a number and add your Athletics bonus:*

- *If 2-6, turn to 113.*
- *If 7-12, turn to 241.*

673

"Did Smithson have any kind of relationship to the Colonel?" you ask. "Was he a former employee or a member of his old regiment, perhaps?"

"No, I doubt that," Sir Andrew answers. "We try to avoid such things — they tend to create problems not in keeping with the atmosphere of our club." *Turn to 119.*

999

You have reached a stumbling block in your investigation — a passage that leads nowhere! Retrace your steps!